1. 熟背「高中
常用7000字」　　　2. 月期考得高分　　　3. 會說流利的英語

1.「用會話背7000字①」書+ CD　280元
以三個極短句為一組的方式，讓同學背了會話，
同時快速增加單字。高一同學要從「國中常用
2000字」挑戰「高中常用7000字」，加強單字是
第一目標。

2.「一分鐘背9個單字」書+ CD　280元
利用字首、字尾的排列，讓你快速增加單字。一次背9個比背
1個字簡單。

3. rival

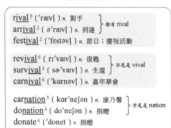

rival⁵ ('raɪvḷ) n. 對手
arrival³ (ə'raɪvḷ) n. 到達　都有 rival
festival² ('fɛstəvḷ) n. 節日；慶祝活動

revival⁶ (rɪ'vaɪvḷ) n. 復甦
survival³ (sə'vaɪvḷ) n. 生還　字尾有 vival
carnival⁶ ('kɑrnəvḷ) n. 嘉年華會

carnation⁵ (kɑr'neʃən) n. 康乃馨
donation⁶ (do'neʃən) n. 捐贈　字尾是 nation
donate⁶ ('donet) v. 捐贈

3.「一口氣考試英語」書+ CD　280元
把大學入學考試題目編成會話，背了以後，
會說英語，又會考試。

例如：

What a nice surprise! (真令人驚喜！)【常考】
I can't believe my eyes.
（我無法相信我的眼睛。）
Little did I dream of seeing you here.
（做夢也沒想到會在這裡看到你。）【駒澤大】

4.「一口氣背文法」書+ CD 280元

英文文法範圍無限大，規則無限多，誰背得完？
劉毅老師把文法整體的概念，編成216句，背完
了會做文法題、會說英語，也會寫作文。既是一
本文法書，也是一本會話書。

1. 現在簡單式的用法

I *get up* early every day.　　　我每天早起。

I *understand* this rule now.　　我現在了解這條規定了。

Actions *speak* louder than
words.　　　　　　　　　　　行動勝於言辭。

【二、三句強調實踐早起】

5.「高中英語聽力測驗①」書+ MP3 280元

6.「高中英語聽力測驗進階」書+ MP3 280元

高一期考聽力佔20%，我們根據大考中心公布的
聽力題型編輯而成。

7.「高一月期考英文試題」書 280元

收集建中、北一女、師大附中、中山、成功、景
美女中等各校試題，並聘請各校名師編寫模擬試
題。

8.「高一英文克漏字測驗」書 180元

9.「高一英文閱讀測驗」書 180元

全部取材自高一月期考試題，英雄
所見略同，重複出現的機率很高。
附有翻譯及詳解，不必查字典，對
錯答案都有明確交待，做完題目，
一看就懂。

高二同學的目標──提早準備考大學

1.「用會話背7000字①②」
書+CD，每冊280元

「用會話背7000字」能夠解決
所有學英文的困難。高二同學
可先從第一冊開始背，第一冊
和第二冊沒有程度上的差異，
背得越多，單字量越多，在腦
海中的短句越多。每一個極短句大多不超過5個字，1個字或
2個字都可以成一個句子，如：「用會話背7000字①」p.184，
每一句都2個字，好背得不得了，而且與生活息息相關，是
每個人都必須知道的知識，例如：成功的祕訣是什麼？

11. What are the keys to success?

Be *ambitious*.	要有**雄心**。
Be *confident*.	要有**信心**。
Have *determination*.	要有**決心**。
Be *patient*.	要有**耐心**。
Be *persistent*.	要有**恆心**。
Show *sincerity*.	要有**誠心**。
Be *charitable*.	要有**愛心**。
Be *modest*.	要**虛心**。
Have *devotion*.	要有**專心**。

當你背單字的時候，就要有「雄心」，要「決心」背好，對
自己要有「信心」，一定要有「耐心」和「恆心」，背書時
要「專心」。

背完後，腦中有2,160個句子，那不得了，無限多的排列組
合，可以寫作文。有了單字，翻譯、閱讀測驗、克漏字都難
不倒你。高二的時候，要下定決心，把7000字背熟、背
爛。雖然高中課本以7000字為範圍，編者為了便宜行事，
往往超出7000字，同學背了少用的單字，反倒忽略真正重要
的單字。千萬記住，背就要背「高中常用7000字」，背完之
後，天不怕、地不怕，任何考試都難不倒你。

2.「時速破百單字快速記憶」書 250元

字尾是 try，重音在倒數第三音節上

> entry³ ('ɛntrɪ) n. 進入【No entry. 禁止進入。】
> country¹ ('kʌntrɪ) n. 國家；鄉下 (ou /ʌ/，為例外字)
> ministry⁴ ('mɪnɪstrɪ) n. 部 (mini = small)
>
> chemistry⁴ ('kɛmɪstrɪ) n. 化學
> geometry⁵ (dʒɪ'ɑmətrɪ) n. 幾何學 (geo 土地，metry 測量)
> industry³ ('ɪndəstrɪ) n. 工業；勤勉 (這個字重音會唸錯)
>
> poetry¹ ('po·ɪtrɪ) n. 詩
> poultry⁴ ('poltrɪ) n. 家禽 ⎫ 字尾是 y 來自「集合名詞」
> pastry⁵ ('pestrɪ) n. 糕餅 ⎭

3.「高二英文克漏字測驗」書 180元

4.「高二英文閱讀測驗」書 180元
　　全部選自各校高二月考試題精華，英雄所見略
　　同，再出現的機率很高。

5.「7000字學測試題詳解」書 250元
　　一般模考題為了便宜行事，往往超出7000字範圍
　　，無論做多少份試題，仍然有大量生字，無法進
　　步。唯有鎖定7000字為範圍的試題，才會對準備
　　考試有幫助。每份試題都經「劉毅英文」同學實
　　際考過，效果奇佳。附有詳細解答，單字標明級
　　數，對錯答案都有明確交待，不需要再查字典，
　　做完題目，再看詳解，快樂無比。

6.「高中常用7000字解析【豪華版】」書 390元
　　按照「大考中心高中英文參考詞彙表」編輯而成
　　。難背的單字有「記憶技巧」、「同義字」及
　　「反義字」，關鍵的單字有「典型考題」。大學
　　入學考試核心單字，以紅色標記。

7.「高中7000字測驗題庫」書 180元
　　取材自大規模考試，解答詳盡，節省查字典的時間。

序 言

　　大學入學考試的單字範圍是高中常用 7000 字，但單字範圍太大，同學背不下來。「升大學必考 1000 字」，將這 7000 字中，國中程度的單字先刪除，再刪除不適合出題目的單字，再統計考試中常考的單字，加上十一個未來考試中，可能出現的關鍵字，相信同學背完之後，不論學校的模擬考試、未來的學力測驗或是指定考試，都能夠得心應手。

　　本書按照單字的詞性編排，分成名詞、動詞、形容詞、副詞等四個部分，完全符合各種大學入學考試詞彙題的測驗目標。同時，為了幫助讀者理解字義及記憶，書中部分單字也加注字根字首分析，如此一來，簡單易背。此外，書

中每隔六頁即附有「自我測驗」及 Check List，可供讀者做自我評量、驗收學習成果之用。

　　本書只有 1000 個單字，再附 1000 個例句，相信在短時間之內就可以溫習完畢。同學們，現在就開始吧！花一點時間，就能夠了解大學入學考試的命題趨勢，何樂而不為呢？

　　這本書是由蔡琇瑩老師，擔任總指揮，外籍老師 Laura 及 Andy 的仔細校對，張家慈小姐和周宛靜小姐協助資料整理，封面由白雪嬌小姐設計，我們感謝大家的辛勞。全書雖經仔細編審校對，但仍恐有疏漏之處，望請讀者不吝批評指正。

劉毅

名 詞

accent (ˈæksɛnt) *n.* 口音

Mr. Tanaka is from Japan and
he speaks English with a
Japanese *accent*. (聯考 49, 86 年，

學測 89 年，指考 102 年)

(p.1～p.83)

access (ˈæksɛs) *n.* 使用權

We have free *access* to the

library. (聯考 68 年，學測 85, 87, 93, 99 年，指考 94, 95, 96, 102 年)

```
ac + cess
 |     |
to  +  go
```

accommodation (əˌkɑməˈdeʃən) *n.* 住宿

When you join a package tour, you don't

have to worry about *accommodation*.

(模考 91 年，聯考 67, 89 年，指考 96 年)

account (əˈkaunt) *n.* 帳戶

My parents opened an *account* for me when

I was seven. (聯考 77, 79, 82 年，學測 90, 92 ①②年，指考 93 ①②年)

acquaintance 〔 ə′kwentəns 〕 *n.*
認識的人

We are only casual *acquaintances*, not close friends. (聯考 55, 61, 66, 68 年)

admiration 〔 ˌædmə′reʃən 〕 *n.* 欽佩

I can only express my *admiration* for his courage. (聯考 47, 64, 68, 72, 74, 79, 84, 87, 88, 89 年，學測 86, 88, 90, 91 ②, 92 ①, 93, 94, 100 年，指考 102 年)

adolescence 〔 ˌædl̩′ɛsn̩s 〕 *n.* 青春期

Adolescence is an important turning point both physically and mentally. (聯考 72 年，學測 92 ①, 96, 99 年，指考 98 年)

advantage 〔 əd′væntɪdʒ 〕 *n.* 優勢

When looking for a job, it's to your *advantage* to speak fluent English.

(聯考 61 年，學測 91 ①②, 92 ②, 101 年，指考 91, 97 年)

adventure ﹝ əd'vɛntʃɚ ﹞ *n.* 冒險

The novel tells the story of a strange and dangerous journey; in other words, it is an *adventure* novel. (學測 90, 91 ①, 100 年，指考 100 年)

advertisement ﹝ ͵ædvɚ'taɪzmənt ﹞ *n.* 廣告

The company put an *advertisement* in the magazine for their new product. (聯考 48, 50, 66, 76, 81, 82 年，學測 84, 88, 96, 99, 101 年，指考 93 ①, 94, 99, 101 年)

affection ﹝ ə'fɛkʃən ﹞ *n.* 感情

No man can be a good teacher unless he has feelings of warm *affection* toward his pupils. (聯考 63, 64, 68, 70, 74, 76, 84 年，學測 83, 88, 91 ①, 93, 97, 98, 101, 102 年，指考 94, 95, 97, 98, 100, 102 年)

agency ﹝ 'edʒənsɪ ﹞ *n.* 代理商

We went on a package tour to Paris arranged by a travel *agency*. (聯考 64, 76 年，學測 85, 92 ②, 96, 99, 101 年，指考 93 ①, 97, 102 年)

allowance 〔 ə'lauəns 〕 *n.* 零用錢

Giving children a proper *allowance* teaches
them to use their money wisely.

alternative 〔 ɔl'tɜnətɪv 〕 *n.* 選擇

They have no *alternative* but to take
part-time jobs. (學測 92 ②, 99, 100 年，指考 98, 100, 101 年)

altitude 〔 'æltə,tjud 〕 *n.* 高度

The plane flew at an
altitude of 30,000
feet. (聯考 63, 65 年，學測 99 年)

alt + itude
| |
high + *n.*

amusement 〔 ə'mjuzmənt 〕 *n.* 娛樂

He hasn't enough money for food, much
less *amusements*. (學測 84, 88, 90 年，指考 91, 97, 101 年)

ancestor 〔 'ænsɛstə 〕 *n.* 祖先

Our *ancestors* have passed down to us a
rich cultural tradition. (聯考 46, 62 年)

anecdote 〔ˈænɪkˌdot〕 *n.* 軼事

An *anecdote* is a brief incident which leads to a humorous climax. (聯考 51 年)

anniversary 〔ˌænəˈvɝsərɪ〕 *n.* 週年紀念

This couple went to Paris to celebrate their tenth wedding *anniversary* last month.

(聯考 46, 62, 88 年，學測 84 年，指考 91, 97 年)

annoyance 〔əˈnɔɪəns〕 *n.* 惱怒

Much to our *annoyance*, he failed to keep his word. (聯考 49, 61, 80, 86 年，學測 90, 101, 102 年，指考 97 年)

appetite 〔ˈæpəˌtaɪt〕 *n.* 食慾

If you have no *appetite*, you don't enjoy the pleasure of eating. (聯考 53, 86 年，學測 91 ②, 101 年)

application 〔ˌæpləˈkeʃən〕 *n.* 申請

If you want to apply for membership in the club, please fill out the *application* form.

(聯考 51, 54, 62, 74, 87 年，學測 85, 88, 91 ①, 94, 100 年，指考 93 ①, 97, 102 年)

appointment 〔 əˈpɔɪntmənt 〕 *n.* 約會

It is considered polite to make an *appointment* before we visit a person or see a doctor. (聯考 49, 54, 69, 81, 89 年，學測 87 年)

aptitude 〔ˈæptəˌtjud 〕 *n.* 性向

John has an *aptitude* for languages. He learns to speak a language in a very short time.

area 〔ˈɛrɪə 〕 *n.* 地區

There is little vegetation in the desert *area*.

(聯考 73, 75, 77, 79, 80, 82, 84 年，學測 83, 87, 93, 94, 96, 97, 98, 100, 102 年，
指考 93 ①②, 94, 95, 97, 99, 100, 101 年)

army 〔ˈɑrmɪ 〕 *n.* 軍隊

It has been his dream to join the *army* since he was young. (聯考 56, 81, 88 年，學測 90, 102 年，指考 102 年)

aspect 〔ˈæspɛkt 〕 *n.* 方面

We must consider all the *aspects* of a problem. (聯考 79, 81 年，指考 94, 102 年)

- [ ] access _____
- [ ] account _____
- [ ] admiration _____
- [ ] advantage _____
- [ ] adventure _____

- [ ] affection _____
- [ ] allowance _____
- [ ] altitude _____
- [ ] amusement _____
- [ ] anniversary _____

- [ ] application _____
- [ ] aptitude _____
- [ ] aspect _____
- [ ] appointment _____
- [ ] agency _____

Check List

1. 口　音　　a ___accent___ t

2. 住　宿　　a _____ n

3. 認識的人　a _____ e

4. 青春期　　a _____ e

5. 廣　告　　a _____ t

6. 選　擇　　a _____ e

7. 約　會　　a _____ t

8. 軍　隊　　a _____ y

9. 食　慾　　a _____ e

10. 冒　險　　a _____ e

11. 欽　佩　　a _____ n

12. 祖　先　　a _____ r

13. 軼　事　　a _____ e

14. 惱　怒　　a _____ e

15. 地　區　　a _____ a

atmosphere〔'ætməs,fɪr〕*n.* 氣氛

We all love the cheerful *atmosphere* of
Christmas. (聯考 53, 60, 61, 80, 82 年，學測 101 年，指考 101 年)

attempt〔ə'tɛmpt〕*n.* 嘗試

George at first had difficulty swimming
across the pool, but he finally succeeded
on his fourth *attempt*. (聯考 49, 56, 65, 66, 81 年，學測 83,
84, 87, 98 年，指考 97, 101 年)

audience〔'ɔdɪəns〕*n.* 聽衆

Hearing the joke, the *audience* broke into
laughter. (聯考 51, 87 年，學測 87, 90,
91 ①②, 100 年，指考 93 ②, 94, 99, 101 年)

authority〔ə'θɔrətɪ〕*n.* 權威

A director in a company has the *authority*
to make decisions. (聯考 51, 65, 78 年，學測 94 年，
指考 92, 93 ①, 98, 100 年)

autograph 〔ˈɔtəˌgræf〕 *n.* 親筆簽名

A lot of fans gathered around the star and asked for his *autograph*. (模考 91 年，學測 83, 91 ② 年)

auto + graph	auto + nomy
| |	| |
self + *write*	*self* + *rule*

autonomy 〔ɔˈtɑnəmɪ〕 *n.* 自治

Often children work for money outside the home as the first step in establishing *autonomy*. (模考 82 年)

awareness 〔əˈwɛrnɪs〕 *n.* 意識

All of us must have the *awareness* that there is no free lunch. (聯考 67, 84, 85 年，學測 101 年)

B b

baggage 〔ˈbægɪdʒ〕 *n.* 行李

She asked the taxi driver to put her *baggage* in the trunk. (學測 92 ① 年)

balance ('bæləns) *n.* 平衡

There is a *balance* between work and play
in his life. (聯考 64, 76, 83, 85, 87 年，學測 98 年)

benefit ('bɛnəfɪt) *n.* 利益

I hope you can take my advice, and get
great *benefit* from reading. (模考 91 年，聯考 67,

85, 89, 90 年，學測 88, 90, 91 ①, 92 ①, 96, 98, 100 年)

bureau ('bjʊro) *n.* 局

This beautiful guidebook is published by
the Tourist *Bureau*. (聯考 60, 64 年，學測 85 年)

C c

candidate ('kændə,det) *n.* 候選人

Among the four *candidates*, we all think
John Smith is the best one. (聯考 85, 89 年，學測 88,

92 ②, 93, 100 年，指考 101, 102 年)

capacity 〔kəˈpæsətɪ〕 *n.* 容量

The theater was filled to *capacity*; there was standing room only. (模考 82 年，聯考 71 年，學測 88, 91 ①, 101 年)

capital 〔ˈkæpətl̩〕 *n.* 首都

Washington, D.C. is the *capital* of the United States of America. (聯考 46, 52, 70, 76 年，學測 87, 94, 97, 99 年，指考 94, 102 年)

career 〔kəˈrɪr〕 *n.* 職業

Nowadays many women would rather pursue their own *careers* than stay at home as housewives. (聯考 50, 51, 60, 63, 69, 74 年，學測 85, 91 ①②, 93, 101 年，指考 91, 93 ①, 94, 95, 97, 98, 99, 101 年)

casualty 〔ˈkæʒʊəltɪ〕 *n.* 死傷人數

The air crash caused a lot of *casualties*; it's really a tragedy. (聯考 69, 80 年)

century (ˈsɛntʃərɪ) *n.* 世紀

The event happened many *centuries* ago.

(聯考 52, 54, 62, 64, 69, 70, 71, 72, 75, 77, 82, 85, 89, 90 年，學測 83, 85, 88, 90, 91 ①,

92 ①, 93, 94, 99, 101, 102 年，指考 92, 93 ①, 94, 97, 100 年)

ceremony (ˈsɛrəˌmonɪ) *n.* 典禮

Jane's wedding *ceremony* will be held on

next Sunday. (聯考 49, 88 年，學測 83, 89, 90, 99 年)

challenge (ˈtʃælɪndʒ) *n.* 挑戰

In this ever changing world, we must be

prepared to face all kinds of *challenges*.

(聯考 66, 69, 77, 90 年，學測 83, 92 ①, 96, 98, 102 年，指考 91, 95, 100, 101 年)

champion (ˈtʃæmpɪən) *n.* 冠軍

It takes rigid training and determination to

be a *champion* in any sport. (模考 91 年)

championship 〔'tʃæmpɪənˌʃɪp 〕 *n.* 冠軍

He won the *championship* in the speech contest. (學測 91 ①, 101 年，指考 92 年)

characteristic 〔ˌkærɪktə'rɪstɪk 〕 *n.* 特質

Always keeping his word is one of his admirable *characteristics*. (聯考 52, 60, 73, 90 年，指考 91, 96 年)

charity 〔'tʃærətɪ 〕 *n.* 慈善

A *charity* sale is held to raise more funds for the orphans. (聯考 56, 61, 68 年，學測 86, 97 年，指考 91, 96, 98 年)

chemistry 〔'kɛmɪstrɪ 〕 *n.* 化學

Dr. Lee Yuan-che was awarded the Nobel Prize for *chemistry* years ago. (聯考 49, 56, 57, 87 年，指考 94 年)

自我測驗

- [ ] authority　　　_____
- [ ] autonomy　　　_____
- [ ] bureau　　　_____
- [ ] awareness　　　_____
- [ ] capacity　　　_____

- [ ] champion　　　_____
- [ ] charity　　　_____
- [ ] attempt　　　_____
- [ ] chemistry　　　_____
- [ ] capital　　　_____

- [ ] balance　　　_____
- [ ] audience　　　_____
- [ ] autograph　　　_____
- [ ] career　　　_____
- [ ] candidate　　　_____

Check List

1. 行　李　　b　*baggage*　e
2. 利　益　　b ＿＿＿＿＿＿＿＿ t
3. 意　識　　a ＿＿＿＿＿＿＿＿ s
4. 候選人　　c ＿＿＿＿＿＿＿＿ e
5. 首　都　　c ＿＿＿＿＿＿＿＿ l

6. 死傷人數　c ＿＿＿＿＿＿＿＿ y
7. 世　紀　　c ＿＿＿＿＿＿＿＿ y
8. 冠　軍　　c ＿＿＿＿＿＿＿＿ p
9. 化　學　　c ＿＿＿＿＿＿＿＿ y
10. 特　質　　c ＿＿＿＿＿＿＿＿ c

11. 氣　氛　　a ＿＿＿＿＿＿＿＿ e
12. 典　禮　　c ＿＿＿＿＿＿＿＿ y
13. 挑　戰　　c ＿＿＿＿＿＿＿＿ e
14. 親筆簽名　a ＿＿＿＿＿＿＿＿ h
15. 聽　衆　　a ＿＿＿＿＿＿＿＿ e

circulation 〔ˌsɝkjəˈleʃən 〕 *n.* 發行量

The newspaper has a large *circulation*.

(學測 96 年，指考 94 年)

circu	+ lat	+ ion
ring	+ *v.*	+ *n.*

climax 〔ˈklaɪmæks 〕 *n.* 高潮

The *climax* of the story was when the dog saved the little girl from the bad man.

(聯考 51, 81 年)

coincidence 〔 koˈɪnsədəns 〕 *n.* 巧合

What a nice surprise! It's really a *coincidence* to meet you here. (聯考 78 年)

colleague 〔ˈkɑlig 〕 *n.* 同事

Due to the help of my *colleagues*, the project was finished successfully. (模考 91 年，

學測 98 年，指考 96 年)

collision 〔 kə'lɪʒən 〕 *n.* 相撞

An airbag is designed to stop the rider from flying forward in the event of a *collision*.

(學測 84 年)

commander 〔 kə'mændɚ 〕 *n.* 指揮官

It is General Bush who acts as *commander* of this operation. (聯考 47 年)

commuter 〔 kə'mjutɚ 〕 *n.* 通勤者

Every morning and evening the subway is packed with *commuters*. (學測 85 年，指考 99 年)

companion 〔 kəm'pænjən 〕 *n.* 同伴

Dogs make good *companions* for human beings. (模考 91 年，聯考 74 年，學測 93, 96 年)

company 〔 'kʌmpənɪ 〕 *n.* 陪伴

I have a cat at home to keep me *company*.

(聯考 90 年，學測 96, 97, 98, 99, 100, 101 年，指考 93 ①②, 94, 97, 99, 100, 102 年)

compassion 〔 kəm'pæʃən 〕 n. 同情

Most of the main religions teach us to have *compassion* for the poor and those who are in need. (聯考 48, 66 年，學測 96, 98 年)

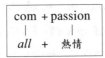

```
com + passion
 |       |
all  +  熱情
```

competition 〔 ‚kɑmpə'tɪʃən 〕 n. 競爭

At the Olympic Games, our representatives are in *competition* with the best athletes from all over the world. (模考 82, 91 年，聯考 77, 89, 90 年，學測 85, 90, 91 ①②, 92 ①, 98, 99, 100, 102 年，指考 91, 93 ①, 95, 97, 99, 101 年)

complaint 〔 kəm'plent 〕 n. 抱怨

The transportation in this city is terrible and people have many *complaints* about it.

(模考 82 年，聯考 48, 54, 61, 62, 65, 80, 82, 84, 86, 88 年，學測 84, 86, 88, 90, 92 ①, 98, 99 年，指考 91, 92, 95 年)

complexion 〔 kəm'plɛkʃən 〕 n. 膚色

She likes to spend her afternoons sunbathing, so she has a tanned *complexion*. （模考 83 年）

concept 〔'kɑnsɛpt 〕 n. 概念

The *concept* of space is developed early in childhood. （聯考 76, 77 年，學測 91 ①②, 99, 101 年，指考 101, 102 年）

concert 〔'kɑnsət 〕 n. 音樂會

All the young people at the rock *concert* danced to the music excitedly. （聯考 48, 54, 87 年，

學測 85, 91 ①年，指考 93 ①②, 102 年）

concession 〔 kən'sɛʃən 〕 n. 讓步

The union refused to offer any *concessions* and threatened to strike.

con	+ cess	+ ion
|	|	|
together	+ *go*	+ *n.*

condition〔kən'dɪʃən〕*n.* 情況

The astronauts have gotten used to the
condition of weightlessness in space.

(聯考 48, 51, 60, 62, 65, 69, 71, 80, 81, 82, 83, 88 年，學測 86, 88, 93, 98, 99 年，

指考 93 ②, 94, 97, 100 年)

conference〔'kɑnfərəns〕*n.* 會議

The director is in *conference* now; you
can see him later. (聯考 66, 68, 69, 73, 87 年，學測 87, 93, 100 年)

confidence〔'kɑnfədəns〕*n.* 信心

He has *confidence* he will win; in other
words, he feels sure he will win. (聯考 48 年，

學測 83 年，指考 91, 97, 98 年)

conflict〔'kɑnflɪkt〕*n.* 衝突

There's always *conflict* between tradition
and innovation. (模考 91 年，聯考 63, 67, 87 年，學測 87, 90,

91 ②, 92 ①, 94, 96, 101 年，指考 91, 96, 97, 99, 101 年)

connection 〔kə'nɛkʃən〕 n. 關聯

He has made a good plan in *connection* with marketing strategies. (模考 91 年，聯考 50, 67, 72, 71, 80, 87 年，學測 84, 86, 87, 89, 91 ②, 92 ②, 94, 96, 97, 100, 101, 102 年，指考 91, 95, 96, 97, 100 年)

conscience 〔'kɑnʃəns〕 n. 良心

I have nothing to be afraid of; I have a clear *conscience*. (模考 91 年，聯考 45, 63, 68 年，指考 91, 99 年)

consciousness 〔'kɑnʃəsnɪs〕 n. 意識

Roger lost *consciousness* and didn't come to until four hours after the accident. (聯考 45 年，學測 91 ①, 94, 101 年，指考 93 ②, 95, 96, 97 年)

consensus 〔kən'sɛnsəs〕 n. 共識

It is of general *consensus* that man should protect the water resources.

自我測驗

- [ ] complexion _____
- [ ] climax _____
- [ ] conflict _____
- [ ] concert _____
- [ ] company _____

- [ ] collision _____
- [ ] companion _____
- [ ] commander _____
- [ ] concession _____
- [ ] commuter _____

- [ ] concept _____
- [ ] condition _____
- [ ] colleague _____
- [ ] compassion _____
- [ ] complaint _____

Check List

1. 共　識　　c＿＿＿*consensus*＿＿＿ s
2. 競　爭　　c＿＿＿＿＿＿＿＿＿＿ n
3. 關　聯　　c＿＿＿＿＿＿＿＿＿＿ n
4. 意　識　　c＿＿＿＿＿＿＿＿＿＿ s
5. 信　心　　c＿＿＿＿＿＿＿＿＿＿ e

6. 情　況　　c＿＿＿＿＿＿＿＿＿＿ n
7. 發行量　　c＿＿＿＿＿＿＿＿＿＿ n
8. 巧　合　　c＿＿＿＿＿＿＿＿＿＿ e
9. 讓　步　　c＿＿＿＿＿＿＿＿＿＿ n
10. 膚　色　　c＿＿＿＿＿＿＿＿＿＿ n

11. 相　撞　　c＿＿＿＿＿＿＿＿＿＿ n
12. 會　議　　c＿＿＿＿＿＿＿＿＿＿ e
13. 良　心　　c＿＿＿＿＿＿＿＿＿＿ e
14. 音樂會　　c＿＿＿＿＿＿＿＿＿＿ t
15. 同　事　　c＿＿＿＿＿＿＿＿＿＿ e

conservation 〔͵kɑnsə′veʃən 〕*n.* 保育

The *conservation* of wildlife needs everybody's cooperation. (聯考 85 年，學測 91 ①,

92 ②年，指考 91, 99 年)

con	+ serv	+ ation
all	+ keep +	*n.*

consideration 〔 kən͵sɪdə′reʃən 〕 *n.* 考慮

Before taking action, we must take into *consideration* the risk of the plan. (聯考 49, 52, 58,

61, 64, 66, 67, 68, 69, 72, 73, 79, 80, 81, 85, 86, 89, 90 年，學測 83, 87, 88, 90, 92 ②,

94, 96, 97, 100, 101, 102 年，指考 91, 92, 93 ①, 95, 97, 99, 100, 101 年)

constitution 〔͵kɑnstə′tjuʃən 〕 *n.* 憲法

The laws of the United States are based on a written *constitution*. (學測 91 ①年，指考 99 年)

construction〔kən'strʌkʃən〕 n. 建造

The *construction* of this bridge will take two years or so. (模考 82 年，聯考 66, 73, 80, 84, 87 年，學測 86, 94, 96, 97 年，指考 91, 92, 93②, 94, 101, 102 年)

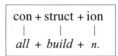

consumption〔kən'sʌmpʃən〕 n. 消耗量

The *consumption* of ice cream increases when summer comes. (聯考 73 年，學測 89, 90, 92②, 96, 97, 99, 100, 102 年，指考 97 年)

contempt〔kən'tɛmpt〕 n. 輕視

Familiarity breeds *contempt*. (聯考 58, 64, 66 年，指考 92 年)

contents〔'kɑntɛnts〕 n. pl. 內容

The customs official opened the suitcase and examined the *contents* of it. (學測 83, 90 年)

contest (ˈkɑntɛst) *n.* 比賽

The winner in the annual singing *contest* will receive a prize of 100,000 dollars.

(聯考 51, 69, 80, 86, 87 年，學測 83, 87, 99, 100, 102 年，指考 91, 96, 97, 100 年)

context (ˈkɑntɛkst) *n.* 上下文

A good reader can often figure out what new words mean by using *context*. (學測 83,

84 年，指考 93 ①, 95 年)

continent (ˈkɑntənənt) *n.* 洲

Asia is the largest *continent* in the world.

(聯考 48, 52 年，學測 91 ① 年)

contrast (ˈkɑntræst) *n.* 對比

Tom is fat and ugly. In *contrast*, his wife is slim and beautiful. (聯考 62, 70, 88 年，學測 85, 87,

91 ②, 99 年，指考 91, 95, 99 年)

contribution 〔͵kɑntrə′bjuʃən 〕 *n.* 貢獻

Women make no less of a *contribution* to the society than men do. (模考 82, 83年，聯考 71, 74, 80, 83, 87年，學測 88, 90, 91 ①, 92 ②, 93, 99年，指考 93 ①, 96, 98, 100, 101, 102年)

con	+ tribut	+ ion
all	+ *give*	+ *n.*

convention 〔 kən′vɛnʃən 〕 *n.* 慣例

It is a *convention* to see a husband as the sole breadwinner. (聯考 90年，學測 99, 101年，指考 93 ②, 95, 98年)

corner 〔′kɔrnɚ 〕 *n.* 轉角

Accidents often happen on narrow roads or on *corners*. (聯考 64年，學測 89, 92 ②年，指考 91, 93 ①年)

counsel 〔′kaʊnsl̩ 〕 *n.* 建議

Mr. Wilson often offers us good *counsel* about our studies or relationships with other people. (聯考 45年)

courtesy 〔ˈkɝtəsɪ〕 *n.* 禮貌

Out of *courtesy* and consideration, I always write a thank-you note when someone sends me a gift. (學測 85 年，指考 96 年)

cradle 〔ˈkredḷ〕 *n.* 搖籃

He tiptoed past the *cradle* lest he should wake up the baby.

crew 〔 kru 〕 *n.* 全體工作人員

All the passengers aboard were killed in the crash, including the *crew*. (聯考 51, 84 年，學測 84 年，指考 92, 101 年)

criminal 〔ˈkrɪmənḷ〕 *n.* 罪犯

The police are searching for the *criminal* who robbed the bank. (聯考 68, 78, 81 年，學測 84, 91 ① 年)

criticism 〔ˈkrɪtəˌsɪzəm 〕 *n.* 批評

Can you offer any constructive *criticism*?

(聯考 54, 66 年，學測 83, 86, 96 年)

curiosity 〔ˌkjʊrɪˈɑsətɪ 〕 *n.* 好奇心

Curiosity killed the cat. (聯考 46, 66, 73 年，學測 84, 85 年)

custom 〔ˈkʌstəm 〕 *n.* 習俗

When visiting a foreign country, we must respect the country's *customs*. (聯考 51, 60 年，

學測 93, 102 年，指考 91, 98, 102 年)

customs 〔ˈkʌstəmz 〕 *n.* 海關

When I passed through *customs*, the officer examined my belongings carefully. (學測 88 年)

cycle 〔ˈsaɪkl̩ 〕 *n.* 週期

The Chinese calendar contains *cycles* of twelve years. (聯考 54, 81, 89 年，學測 88, 98, 100 年)

自 我 測 驗

- [ ] contrast   _____
- [ ] custom   _____
- [ ] cradle   _____
- [ ] crew   _____
- [ ] conservation   _____

- [ ] cycle   _____
- [ ] counsel   _____
- [ ] continent   _____
- [ ] contempt   _____
- [ ] courtesy   _____

- [ ] constitution   _____
- [ ] contents   _____
- [ ] convention   _____
- [ ] criminal   _____
- [ ] customs   _____

Check List

1.	轉　角	c _____*corner*_____	r
2.	輕　視	c _____	t
3.	貢　獻	c _____	n
4.	比　賽	c _____	t
5.	批　評	c _____	m
6.	建　造	c _____	n
7.	好奇心	c _____	y
8.	禮　貌	c _____	y
9.	上下文	c _____	t
10.	憲　法	c _____	n
11.	消耗量	c _____	n
12.	習　俗	c _____	m
13.	內　容	c _____	s
14.	海　關	c _____	s
15.	考　慮	c _____	n

D d

declaration 〔͵dɛklə'reʃən〕 *n.* 宣言

The Americans signed the *Declaration* of Independence on July 4 in 1776. (模考 83 年，

聯考 58 年，學測 88, 89, 93 年)

defense 〔 dɪ'fɛns 〕 *n.* 防禦

Every country needs strong national *defense* against enemy invasions. (聯考 47, 65, 73,

85, 89 年，學測 96, 97 年)

definition 〔͵dɛfə'nɪʃən〕 *n.* 定義

If you don't know what a word means, look in the dictionary for its *definition*. (聯考 48, 55, 72,

73, 78, 83, 87, 88, 89 年，學測 85, 90, 92 ①, 94, 97 年，指考 92, 94, 98 年)

degree 〔 dɪ'gri 〕 *n.* 學位

Applicants for the job must have a *degree* in engineering. (聯考 45, 50, 54, 61, 67, 69, 70, 72, 84, 85 年，

學測 88, 91 ②, 94, 100 年，指考 91, 93 ①, 100, 102 年)

demand 〔 dɪ'mænd 〕 *n.* 需求

Men to shovel snow were in great *demand* after the snowstorm. (聯考 50, 51, 54, 58, 59, 61, 64, 66, 73, 86, 87, 89 年，學測 89, 90, 91 ②, 94, 97, 100, 102 年，指考 98, 99, 100, 102 年)

demonstration 〔 ˌdɛmən'streʃən 〕 *n.* 示範

The salesman gave a *demonstration* of the new personal computer. (聯考 69, 88 年，學測 90, 91 ①, 94 年，指考 91, 94, 95 年)

departure 〔 dɪ'pɑrtʃɚ 〕 *n.* 離開

The *departure* of the plane was delayed for an hour due to heavy fog. (聯考 66, 71, 86, 88 年，學測 86, 92 ②, 99 年)

depreciation 〔 dɪˌpriʃɪ'eʃən 〕 *n.* 貶值

The inflation led to the *depreciation* of the currency.

de	+ preci	+ ation
|	|	|
down	+ *price* +	*n.*

depression〔dɪˋprɛʃən〕*n.* 沮喪

His *depression* came to an end when she kissed him. (聯考 50, 68, 81, 88 年，學測 84, 86, 87, 92 ①, 94, 97, 101 年，指考 91, 96, 98, 101 年)

descendant〔dɪˋsɛndənt〕*n.* 子孫

The people living in the village are said to be the *descendants* of Italians. (聯考 58, 62, 71 年)

description〔dɪˋskrɪpʃən〕*n.* 敘述

The beauty of the English countryside is beyond *description*. (模考 83 年，聯考 59, 62, 73, 76, 78, 81, 84, 85, 88 年，學測 85, 87, 88, 91 ①, 92 ①, 93, 98, 99, 101 年，指考 91, 94, 96, 98, 99 年)

```
de    + script + ion
 |        |       |
down  + write  +  n.
```

despair〔dɪˋspɛr〕*n.* 絕望

A string of failures drove him to *despair*.

(聯考 56, 61, 72 年，指考 91 年)

destination 〔͵dɛstə'neʃən〕 *n.* 目的地

The plane departed for its next *destination* on time. (學測 87, 91 ①, 98 年，指考 94 年)

destruction 〔 dɪ'strʌkʃən 〕 *n.* 破壞

The *destruction* caused by a war cannot be estimated. (模考 82 年，聯考 48, 67, 71, 85, 87, 90 年，學測 89, 97, 102 年，指考 91, 93 ①, 101 年)

determination 〔 dɪ͵tɝmə'neʃən 〕 *n.* 決心

A person of great *determination* usually can achieve his goal. (聯考 47, 53, 69, 71, 77, 84, 86, 88 年，學測 85, 86, 90, 91 ②, 92 ②, 96, 102 年，指考 91, 101 年)

dialect 〔'daɪəlɛkt 〕 *n.* 方言

Taiwanese and Cantonese are both *dialects* of Chinese. (聯考 76 年，學測 102 年，指考 99 年)

dialogue〔'daɪə,lɔg〕*n.* 對話

They are practicing those
English *dialogues* in class.

dia	+	logue
two	+	speak

(聯考 75 年)

dignity〔'dɪgnətɪ〕*n.* 尊嚴

A man's *dignity* depends not upon his
wealth or rank but upon his character.

(模考 82 年，聯考 53, 69, 90 年，學測 88 年，指考 91, 93 ① 年)

diligence〔'dɪlədʒəns〕*n.* 勤勉

Diligence is one of the ingredients of his
success. (聯考 53, 71, 73, 74, 83 年，學測 98, 101 年，指考 99 年)

diploma〔dɪ'plomə〕*n.* 文憑

You have to undergo several examinations
before you get your *diploma*.

(聯考 70 年，學測 88 年)

disciple 〔 dɪ'saɪpl̩ 〕 *n.* 弟子

Confucius attracted many *disciples* when he began teaching. (模考 83 年，聯考 71 年，學測 97 年)

discipline 〔'dɪsəplɪn 〕 *n.* 紀律

The children were clever, but lacked *discipline*. (模考 83 年，學測 85, 91 ②, 92 ②年，指考 99 年)

discount 〔'dɪskaʊnt 〕 *n.* 折扣

If you pay in cash, you can have a ten percent *discount*.

(聯考 89 年，學測 102 年，指考 96 年)

```
dis + count
 |      |
not +  計算
```

dismay 〔 dɪs'me 〕 *n.* 驚慌

To his *dismay*, Tom realized he had left his bags on the bus. (聯考 63 年)

- ☐ dialect _____
- ☐ degree _____
- ☐ despair _____
- ☐ dignity _____
- ☐ disciple _____

- ☐ defense _____
- ☐ descendant _____
- ☐ departure _____
- ☐ destination _____
- ☐ discipline _____

- ☐ dismay _____
- ☐ discount _____
- ☐ demand _____
- ☐ declaration _____
- ☐ diploma _____

Check List

1. 對　話　　d_____*dialogue*_____ e

2. 紀　律　　d _____ e

3. 勤　勉　　d _____ e

4. 決　心　　d _____ n

5. 定　義　　d _____ n

6. 示　範　　d _____ n

7. 目的地　　d _____ n

8. 敘　述　　d _____ n

9. 破　壞　　d _____ n

10. 宣　言　　d _____ n

11. 折　扣　　d _____ t

12. 沮　喪　　d _____ n

13. 驚　慌　　d _____ y

14. 貶　值　　d _____ n

15. 子　孫　　d _____ t

display (dɪ'sple) *n.* 展示

The collection of Picasso's paintings was on *display* in the museum. (聯考 62, 74, 84, 88, 90 年,

學測 84, 90, 99, 100, 102 年,指考 93 ②, 94, 95 年)

disposal (dɪ'spozl) *n.* 處理

Garbage *disposal* is a major issue for the city government. (聯考 84 年,學測 86, 92 ② 年)

dispute (dɪ'spjut) *n.* 爭論

The union and the management are in *dispute* over working conditions. (模考 91 年,

聯考 75, 84 年,學測 87, 90 年,指考 99 年)

distribution (ˌdɪstrə'bjuʃən) *n.* 分配

The *distribution* of the world population has changed during the last centuries.

(聯考 60, 63, 75, 85 年,學測 92 ②, 93, 96, 102 年,指考 102 年)

dis	+ tribut	+ ion
apart	+ *give*	+ *n.*

disturbance 〔 dɪ'stɝbəns 〕 *n.* 騷擾

The noise outside is really a *disturbance*.
I can't stand it any more. (聯考 61, 64, 69, 78, 87, 90 年，

學測 83, 87, 90, 94 年，指考 94, 96 年)

drain 〔 dren 〕 *n.* 排水管

I failed despite everything I did. All my
efforts went down the *drain*. (聯考 70 年)

drawback 〔'drɔ,bæk 〕 *n.* 缺點

Living in a big house has advantages as
well as *drawbacks*. (學測 98 年)

drought 〔 draʊt 〕 *n.* 乾旱

Tens of thousands of Africans died in the
drought for lack of water. (聯考 63, 73, 87, 89 年)

E e

eclipse 〔 ɪ'klɪps 〕 *n.* (日、月) 蝕

According to the astronomers, a solar
eclipse is to happen next month.

economy 〔 ɪ'kɑnəmɪ 〕 *n.* 經濟

The *economy* of our nation will surely turn
for the better. (聯考 70, 76, 78, 83, 85 年，學測 88, 98 年，指考 95,
96 年)

edge 〔 ɛdʒ 〕 *n.* 邊緣

At the *edge* of the brook, some women
were washing clothes. (聯考 67, 90 年，指考 91, 94, 99 年)

edition 〔 ɪ'dɪʃən 〕 *n.* 版本

The latest *edition* of this dictionary sells
well.

editor 〔ˈɛdɪtɚ〕 *n.* 編輯

He was promoted to *editor* in chief of the publishing company. (聯考 61 年,學測 88, 96 年,指考 93 ②, 99 年)

effect 〔ɪˈfɛkt〕 *n.* 影響

His mother's attitude toward him has a great *effect* on him. (聯考 48, 63, 67, 68, 70, 71, 72, 80, 81, 83, 84, 88, 90 年,學測 83, 85, 87, 92 ①②, 93, 96, 97, 98, 99, 101 年,指考 91, 92, 93 ①②, 94, 95, 96, 98, 99, 100, 102 年)

elevator 〔ˈɛləˌvetɚ〕 *n.* 電梯

The building is ten stories high with two *elevators*. (聯考 72 年,學測 83, 92 ①年,指考 92 年)

emergency 〔ɪˈmɝdʒənsɪ〕 *n.* 緊急情況

We always keep a fire extinguisher for use in case of an *emergency*. (聯考 48, 51, 68 年,學測 83, 93 年,指考 93 ①年)

emphasis ('ɛmfəsɪs) *n.* 強調

You place too much *emphasis* on money.
Money is important, but it's not everything.

(聯考 66, 69, 73, 88 年,學測 88, 97, 98, 99, 102 年,指考 93 ①, 95 年)

encouragement (ɪn'kɝɪdʒmənt) *n.* 鼓勵

A little *encouragement* often brings out
the best in even the most stubborn child.

(聯考 49, 76, 73, 80, 82, 83, 87, 88 年,學測 83, 84, 85, 86, 87, 91 ②, 94, 96 年,
指考 91, 92, 93 ②, 95, 96, 98, 100, 102 年)

en	+	courage	+	ment
in	+	勇氣	+	*n.*

entertainment (ˌɛntɚ'tenmənt) *n.* 娛樂

Movies, sports and reading are forms of
entertainment. They help us relax. (聯考 48, 50,
63, 73, 82, 90 年,學測 88, 92 ①, 94, 96, 100, 102 年,指考 91, 97, 101 年)

enthusiasm 〔 ɪn'θjuzɪˌæzəm 〕 *n.* 熱衷

He has a great *enthusiasm* for professional baseball. (模考 82 年，聯考 47, 53, 66, 90 年，學測 83, 88, 91 ② 年，指考 91, 93 ①, 94, 95 年)

equipment 〔 ɪ'kwɪpmənt 〕 *n.* 裝備

The whole set of office *equipment* cost a lot of money. (聯考 47, 78 年，學測 83, 86, 88, 90, 94, 101, 102 年，指考 91, 93 ②, 95, 99 年)

eruption 〔 ɪ'rʌpʃən 〕 *n.* 爆發

Volcanic *eruptions* will influence the global weather patterns. (聯考 71 年)

$$
\begin{array}{ccc}
e & + \text{ rupt } & + \text{ ion} \\
| & | & | \\
out & + \ break & + \quad n.
\end{array}
$$

esteem 〔 ə'stim 〕 *n.* 尊重

Americans hold independence and individualism in high *esteem*. (模考 82 年，聯考 66 年，指考 96 年)

自 我 測 驗

- [ ] edge　　　　　＿＿＿＿＿＿＿＿＿＿
- [ ] esteem　　　　＿＿＿＿＿＿＿＿＿＿
- [ ] drain　　　　　＿＿＿＿＿＿＿＿＿＿
- [ ] eclipse　　　　＿＿＿＿＿＿＿＿＿＿
- [ ] effect　　　　　＿＿＿＿＿＿＿＿＿＿

- [ ] disposal　　　＿＿＿＿＿＿＿＿＿＿
- [ ] elevator　　　＿＿＿＿＿＿＿＿＿＿
- [ ] eruption　　　＿＿＿＿＿＿＿＿＿＿
- [ ] edition　　　　＿＿＿＿＿＿＿＿＿＿
- [ ] drought　　　＿＿＿＿＿＿＿＿＿＿

- [ ] emphasis　　　＿＿＿＿＿＿＿＿＿＿
- [ ] editor　　　　　＿＿＿＿＿＿＿＿＿＿
- [ ] dispute　　　　＿＿＿＿＿＿＿＿＿＿
- [ ] equipment　　＿＿＿＿＿＿＿＿＿＿
- [ ] disturbance　　＿＿＿＿＿＿＿＿＿＿

Check List

1. 缺　　點　　　d _drawback_ k
2. 娛　　樂　　　e ＿＿＿＿＿＿＿ t
3. 分　　配　　　d ＿＿＿＿＿＿＿ n
4. 熱　　衷　　　e ＿＿＿＿＿＿＿ m
5. 騷　　擾　　　d ＿＿＿＿＿＿＿ e

6. 鼓　　勵　　　e ＿＿＿＿＿＿＿ t
7. 經　　濟　　　e ＿＿＿＿＿＿＿ y
8. 爭　　論　　　d ＿＿＿＿＿＿＿ e
9. 展　　示　　　d ＿＿＿＿＿＿＿ y
10. 強　　調　　　e ＿＿＿＿＿＿＿ s

11. 緊急情況　　　e ＿＿＿＿＿＿＿ y
12. 爆　　發　　　e ＿＿＿＿＿＿＿ n
13. 處　　理　　　d ＿＿＿＿＿＿＿ l
14. 影　　響　　　e ＿＿＿＿＿＿＿ t
15. 編　　輯　　　e ＿＿＿＿＿＿＿ r

evidence ('ɛvədəns) *n.* 證據

The case has been dismissed for lack of *evidence*. (聯考 71, 72, 76, 78, 89 年，學測 84, 92 ② 年，指考 95, 100 年)

exception (ɪk'sɛpʃən) *n.* 例外

There's an *exception* to every rule. (聯考 47, 49, 59, 64, 70, 71, 75, 79, 83, 85, 86, 87, 89, 90 年，學測 88, 89, 91 ①, 100, 101 年，指考 91, 94, 95, 96, 99, 102 年)

exchange (ɪks'tʃendʒ) *n.* 交換

Nowadays there are more and more *exchange* students between Taiwan and the U.S. (聯考 53, 54, 67, 68, 78, 87, 89, 90 年，學測 86, 89, 91 ②, 98, 99 年，指考 91, 93 ①, 100 年)

exhibition (,ɛksə'bɪʃən) *n.* 展覽會

Have you seen the art *exhibition* at the Palace Museum? (聯考 49, 66, 68, 85, 89 年，學測 87, 90, 101 年，指考 99, 101 年)

expansion〔ɪkˈspænʃən〕 *n.* 擴張

The *expansion* of this empire led to many wars with its neighboring countries. (聯考 83, 84, 86 年，學測 88, 93, 94, 96 年，指考 93 ①, 97, 98, 100, 102 年)

expectation〔ˌɛkspɛkˈteʃən〕 *n.* 期望

It is difficult for a son to always live up to the *expectations* of his parents.

(模考 91 年，聯考 49, 58, 61, 62, 66, 67, 68, 71, 79, 80, 81, 83, 89, 90 年，學測 84, 87, 91 ②, 92 ②, 94, 96, 97, 98, 99, 101 年，指考 91, 92, 93 ②, 94, 95, 98, 100, 102 年)

expense〔ɪkˈspɛns〕 *n.* 費用

I've had some extra *expenses* this month and it's been hard to make both ends meet.

(聯考 58, 68, 80, 86, 88, 90 年，學測 96 年，指考 100, 102 年)

experiment〔ɪkˈspɛrəmənt〕 *n.* 實驗

They are doing a biological *experiment* in the lab. (模考 83, 91 年，聯考 48, 49, 50, 60, 62, 65, 66, 71, 77, 79, 82, 87, 88 年，學測 97, 100, 102 年，指考 92, 95, 99, 100 年)

explanation 〔͵ɛksplə'neʃən 〕 *n.* 解釋

The case is very clear and we don't need further *explanation.* (聯考 57, 61, 63, 76, 77, 80, 85, 86, 88, 89 年,

學測 89, 90, 91 ①②, 92 ①②, 94, 96, 98, 100, 102 年,指考 92, 94, 99, 100, 101 年)

exposure 〔 ɪk'spoʒɚ 〕 *n.* 暴露

Too much *exposure* to the sunlight may cause skin cancer.

(聯考 50, 57, 62, 68 年,學測 86, 90,

92 ②, 98, 99 年,指考 98, 101 年)

```
ex + pos + ure
 |     |     |
out + put +  n.
```

expression 〔 ɪk'sprɛʃən 〕 *n.* 表達

The beauty of this mountain scene is beyond *expression.* (聯考 65, 67, 72, 73, 79, 84, 85, 87, 88, 90 年,學測 85, 86, 88,

91 ①, 92 ①②, 93, 94, 96, 99, 100, 101 年,指考 91, 93 ①, 97, 98, 99, 100, 102 年)

```
ex + press + ion
 |     |      |
out +  壓  +  n.
```

extent 〔 ɪk'stɛnt 〕 *n.* 程度

I really don't know to what *extent* we can trust him. (聯考 81 年，學測 90 年)

extravagance 〔 ɪk'strævəgəns 〕 *n.* 浪費

You should spend your money carefully and avoid *extravagance*. (聯考 63 年)

F f

fable 〔'febḷ 〕 *n.* 寓言

Many *fables* contain such characters as talking animals and magical witches.

(學測 91 ②, 98 年，指考 92 年)

factor 〔'fæktɚ 〕 *n.* 因素

Humility is an important *factor* in his success. (聯考 47, 52, 64, 78, 85, 87 年，學測 91 ②, 92 ②, 98, 99, 102 年，指考 93 ②, 94 年)

failure (ˈfeljə) *n.* 失敗

The *failure* of the project disappointed the scientists. (聯考 50, 51, 52, 60, 65, 67, 71, 87 年，學測 90, 98 年，指考 91, 93 ② 年)

faith (feθ) *n.* 信任

Husband and wife must have *faith* in each other. (聯考 71, 87 年，學測 92 ① 年)

favor (ˈfevə) *n.* 恩惠

Would you please do me a *favor*? (聯考 63, 64, 66, 76, 81 年，學測 91 ①, 92 ②, 101, 102 年，指考 91, 97 年)

feather (ˈfɛðə) *n.* 羽毛

Birds of a *feather* flock together. (聯考 50 年)

feature (ˈfitʃə) *n.* 特色

My apartment has one *feature* I like. It has a fireplace in the living room. (聯考 64, 71, 77, 81, 83, 88 年，學測 84, 90, 91 ②, 92 ①, 97, 98, 101 年，指考 94, 97, 98, 99, 101 年)

fiction〔'fɪkʃən〕*n.* 小說

Fact is sometimes stranger than *fiction*.

(聯考 50, 81 年，學測 91 ① 年，指考 91, 102 年)

figure〔'fɪgɚ〕*n.* 數字

He has an income of six *figures*. (聯考 50, 65, 70, 73, 75, 81 年，學測 84, 88, 101 年，指考 91, 93 ① ②, 94, 95, 96, 97, 100, 101, 102 年)

flavor〔'flevɚ〕*n.* 口味

The store sells thirty-one *flavors* of ice cream. (聯考 52 年，學測 93, 97, 99, 100 年，指考 99, 100 年)

flock〔flɑk〕*n.* 一群

A *flock* of migrant birds flew to our island yesterday. (聯考 84, 85 年，學測 91 ②, 102 年，指考 93 ① 年)

forecast〔'for͵kæst〕*n.* 預測

Weathermen use scientific instruments to make *forecasts*. (聯考 76 年，指考 91 年)

```
fore  + cast
  |       |
before + throw（先把消息丟出來）
```

自我測驗

- [ ] favor _____
- [ ] flavor _____
- [ ] evidence _____
- [ ] fable _____
- [ ] extent _____

- [ ] feather _____
- [ ] exposure _____
- [ ] exchange _____
- [ ] factor _____
- [ ] expense _____

- [ ] figure _____
- [ ] flock _____
- [ ] expression _____
- [ ] feature _____
- [ ] exception _____

1. 小　說　　f _____fiction_____ n
2. 信　任　　f _____ h
3. 特　色　　f _____ e
4. 期　望　　e _____ n
5. 展覽會　　e _____ n

6. 解　釋　　e _____ n
7. 浪　費　　e _____ e
8. 擴　張　　e _____ n
9. 預　測　　f _____ t
10. 失　敗　　f _____ e

11. 實　驗　　e _____ t
12. 例　外　　e _____ n
13. 暴　露　　e _____ e
14. 程　度　　e _____ t
15. 口　味　　f _____ r

fortune ('fɔrtʃən) *n.* 財富

Julia made a *fortune* in the lottery. (聯考 45, 47,

74 年，學測 86, 96, 100, 102 年，指考 93 ①, 96, 100 年)

foundation (faʊn'deʃən) *n.* 基礎

A good system of knowledge is the
foundation of democracy. (模考 91 年，聯考 51, 52, 69,

72, 87 年，學測 92 ①, 96 年，指考 93 ②, 98, 102 年)

founder ('faʊndɚ) *n.* 創始人

The *founder* of the American Red Cross
was Clara Barton. (聯考 76 年，指考 93 ①, 101 年)

fragrance ('fregrəns) *n.* 芳香

The *fragrance* of flowers pervades the
garden. (聯考 71 年，學測 84, 97, 98 年，指考 94 年)

fright (fraɪt) *n.* 害怕

I suffered from stage *fright* when I was
little. I was afraid to talk in public. (聯考 62 年)

fulfillment 〔 fʊlˈfɪlmənt 〕 *n.* 實現

When I became a college student, it was the *fulfillment* of all my dreams. (聯考 68, 88, 89 年,

學測 91 ①, 94 年,指考 93 ① 年)

function 〔ˈfʌŋkʃən 〕 *n.* 功能

The *function* of a hammer is to hit nails into wood. (聯考 51, 67, 75, 78, 81, 85, 87, 89 年,學測 87, 97, 100,

102 年,指考 91, 96, 97, 100 年)

G g

generosity 〔ˌdʒɛnəˈrɑsətɪ 〕 *n.* 慷慨

We are grateful for his *generosity* in giving a large contribution to our foundation.

(聯考 61, 63, 69, 82, 85, 87, 89 年,學測 86, 88, 83, 90, 96 年,指考 92, 97, 102 年)

gratitude 〔ˈgrætəˌtjud 〕 *n.* 感激

Thank you so much. I really don't know how to express my *gratitude* to you.

(模考 82 年,指考 93 ① 年)

greed〔grid〕*n.* 貪心

His *greed* for power led him to tragedy.

(模考 82 年，聯考 85, 86, 90 年，學測 91 ② 年，指考 98 年)

grocery〔'grosərɪ〕*n.* 食品雜貨店

I went to the *grocery* store to buy some
sugar for my mom. (聯考 71, 79, 83, 89 年，指考 95 年)

H h

harvest〔'hɑrvɪst〕*n.* 收穫

Due to good weather, the farmers had a
good *harvest* this year. (聯考 75 年，學測 94, 97, 99 年，

指考 93 ①, 99, 100 年)

haste〔hest〕*n.* 匆忙

An old saying goes, "More *haste*, less
speed." (聯考 64, 88 年，指考 100 年)

headline ('hɛd,laɪn) *n.* 標題

The incident appeared in the newspaper *headlines*. Everybody knew about it.

(學測 83 年，指考 94 年)

heredity (hə'rɛdətɪ) *n.* 遺傳

The color of our skin is due to *heredity*.

(模考 91 年，聯考 78 年)

heritage ('hɛrətɪdʒ) *n.* 遺產

The millionaire's *heritage* will all go to the orphanage after his death. (模考 91 年，聯考 64, 69, 70 年，學測 97, 101 年，指考 102 年)

hesitation (,hɛzə'teʃən) *n.* 猶豫

He is a man of resolution. He always makes his decisions without *hesitation*. (聯考 64, 69, 86, 90 年，學測 87, 91 ①, 96, 97, 99, 101 年，指考 95, 96 年)

honor (ˈɑnɚ) *n.* 尊敬

We celebrate Teachers' Day in *honor* of
Confucius. (聯考 68, 72, 79, 82, 84 年，學測 83, 88, 96, 97 年，
指考 92, 93 ①, 94, 99, 101 年)

horror (ˈhɑrɚ) *n.* 恐怖

She recoiled in *horror* at the sight of the
snake. (聯考 68 年，指考 100 年)

humanity (hjuˈmænətɪ) *n.* 人類

Each nation contributes something to the
fullness of the life of *humanity*. (聯考 87 年，
學測 86 年，指考 95, 98, 100 年)

humility (hjuˈmɪlətɪ) *n.* 謙遜

The girl has the great virtues of *humility*
and kindliness. (模考 82 年)

hypothesis 〔 haɪˈpɑθəsɪs 〕 *n.* 假設

His theory is based on the *hypothesis* that all men are born equal. (模考 83 年，聯考 87 年，指考 100 年)

I i

identity 〔 aɪˈdɛntətɪ 〕 *n.* 身分

The *identity* of the dead body has not been confirmed. (學測 88, 99 年，指考 98 年)

ignorance 〔ˈɪgnərəns 〕 *n.* 無知

He failed again because of his *ignorance*.

(聯考 54, 62, 69, 73, 86, 89 年，指考 99 年)

image 〔ˈɪmɪdʒ 〕 *n.* 形象

The *image* I have of the principal is that of a very kind and gentle person. (聯考 56, 80, 81, 84 年，

學測 90, 91 ②, 94, 98, 99 年，指考 94, 95 年)

自 我 測 驗

- [ ] greed   _____
- [ ] honor   _____
- [ ] image   _____
- [ ] identity   _____
- [ ] haste   _____

- [ ] fright   _____
- [ ] horror   _____
- [ ] function   _____
- [ ] heredity   _____
- [ ] humanity   _____

- [ ] headline   _____
- [ ] founder   _____
- [ ] fortune   _____
- [ ] grocery   _____
- [ ] hypothesis   _____

Check List

1. 芳　香	f	_fragrance_	e
2. 感　激	g		e
3. 收　穫	h		t
4. 尊　敬	h		r
5. 無　知	i		e
6. 遺　傳	h		y
7. 慷　慨	g		y
8. 實　現	f		t
9. 基　礎	f		n
10. 假　設	h		s
11. 猶　豫	h		n
12. 謙　遜	h		y
13. 財　富	f		e
14. 人　類	h		y
15. 遺　產	h		e

imagination 〔 ˌɪˌmædʒə'neʃən 〕 *n.* 想像力

His composition, which was full of
imagination, won his teacher's approval.

(聯考 49, 67, 68, 69, 70, 81, 84, 86, 87, 88, 90 年，學測 90, 91 ①②, 93 年，

指考 91, 96, 97, 100 年)

immunity 〔 ɪ'mjunətɪ 〕 *n.* 免疫

Regular exercise boosts one's *immunity*
to colds. (學測 97 年，指考 94 年)

impact 〔 'ɪmpækt 〕 *n.* 影響

Parents' attitude has a great *impact* on
children's growth. (聯考 83 年，學測 85, 86, 91 ①, 98 年，

指考 93 ②, 94, 100, 101 年)

impression 〔 ɪm'prɛʃən 〕 *n.* 印象

When you went to Tokyo, what made the
deepest *impression* on you?

(模考 91 年，聯考 62, 66, 69, 73, 79, 84,

86, 88 年，學測 84, 88, 91 ①, 92 ①, 94,

98, 101 年，指考 94 年)

im	+	press	+	ion
in	+	壓	+	*n.*

imprisonment 〔 ɪm'prɪznmənt 〕 *n.* 監禁

He was sentenced to life *imprisonment* by the judge. (模考 91 年，聯考 78 年)

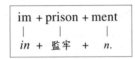

im	+	prison	+	ment
in	+	監牢	+	*n.*

improvement 〔 ɪm'pruvmənt 〕 *n.* 改善

There has been significant *improvement* in the traffic and living conditions in Taipei.

(模考 91 年，聯考 49, 62, 64, 69, 70, 71, 77, 81, 83, 87, 90 年，學測 83, 91 ①②，98 年，指考 92, 93 ②, 94, 97, 99, 100, 101, 102 年)

impulse 〔 'ɪmpʌls 〕 *n.* 衝動

Many people are guided by *impulse* rather than by reason. (聯考 64, 89 年，學測 93 年，指考 96 年)

incident 〔 'ɪnsədənt 〕 *n.* 事件

He told me of a strange *incident* during his journey. (聯考 51, 62, 64, 66, 78, 83 年，學測 86, 93, 94, 96, 99 年，指考 92, 101, 102 年)

independence (ˌɪndɪˈpɛndəns) *n.* 獨立

On July 4, the Americans celebrate their
independence from Britain. (聯考 51, 53, 55, 65, 69, 72,

80, 86 年，指考 93①, 97, 101 年)

in	+ depend	+ ence
not +	依賴 +	*n.*

index (ˈɪndɛks) *n.* 索引

If you can't find what you want in the
book, look it up in the *index*.

indication (ˌɪndəˈkeʃən) *n.* 跡象

There are many *indications* that the
economy will recover from the recession.

(聯考 49, 69, 73, 83, 84, 86, 88 年，學測 83, 85, 89, 93, 102 年，指考 92, 98, 100 年)

indifference (ɪnˈdɪfrəns) *n.* 漠不關心

City people are showing more *indifference*
to the suffering of their neighbors. (聯考 57, 60, 67,

69, 75, 85, 86 年，學測 94 年，指考 95, 96, 99, 100, 102 年)

industry (ˈɪndəstrɪ) *n.* 工業

The country's revenue depends mainly on its tourist *industry*. (聯考 56, 61, 63, 64, 83, 87 年，學測 86, 88, 91 ①, 96, 98, 101 年，指考 91, 93 ①, 95, 98, 102 年)

information (ˌɪnfəˈmeʃən) *n.* 資訊

With mass media, we can acquire various kinds of *information*. (聯考 69, 72, 73, 76, 78, 81, 86, 87, 88 年，學測 85, 86, 88, 92 ①②, 94, 98, 99, 101, 102 年，指考 92, 94, 95, 99, 100, 101 年)

```
in + form + ation
 |     |      |
in + 形成  +  n. (在心中造形)
```

ingredient (ɪnˈɡridɪənt) *n.* 成分

That's the most important *ingredient* in the recipe. (聯考 89 年，學測 91 ②, 93 年)

initiative (ɪˈnɪʃɪˌetɪv) *n.* 主動

Jane always takes the *initiative*. She takes the necessary action and does not wait for orders. (指考 91, 95 年)

injection〔ɪn'dʒɛkʃən〕 *n.* 注射

The nurse gave him an *injection* to relieve his pain.

in	+	ject	+ ion
in	+	throw	+ *n.*

in	+	spir	+ ation
in	+	breathe	+ *n.*

inspiration〔ˌɪnspə'reʃən〕 *n.* 靈感

Many poets and writers drew their *inspiration* from nature. (模考 82 年，聯考 47, 64, 72, 73, 87 年，學測 86, 90, 97, 101 年，指考 92, 98, 99, 101, 102 年)

instance〔'ɪnstəns〕 *n.* 例子

She likes sweets. For *instance*, chocolate is her favorite. (學測 84, 85, 97, 101 年，指考 92, 93 ②, 94, 95, 99, 101 年)

instinct〔'ɪnstɪŋkt〕 *n.* 本能

Humans learn by experience, whereas animals' behavior depends mainly on *instinct*. (聯考 64 年，學測 100 年，指考 99 年)

instruction〔 ɪnˈstrʌkʃən 〕 *n.* 指示

Follow the *instructions* closely, and you will find it easy to assemble the bicycle.

(聯考 65, 71, 72, 73 , 75, 83, 86, 87 年，學測 86, 87, 97 年，指考 93 ①, 96 年)

in	+ struct	+ ion
in	+ *build*	+ *n.*

instrument〔ˈɪnstrəmənt 〕 *n.* 樂器

Sharon can play several kinds of *instruments*, such as the piano and violin.

(聯考 51, 65, 68, 81, 82 年，學測 92 ①, 98, 100 年)

intelligence〔 ɪnˈtɛlədʒəns 〕 *n.* 智力

The monkey has the *intelligence* of a five-year-old child. (聯考 49, 52, 63, 65, 71, 73, 74, 81, 83 年，

學測 87, 100, 102 年，指考 93 ①, 94, 96 年)

自我測驗

- [ ] index _____
- [ ] impulse _____
- [ ] incident _____
- [ ] instance _____
- [ ] immunity _____

- [ ] instinct _____
- [ ] initiative _____
- [ ] industry _____
- [ ] injection _____
- [ ] impression _____

- [ ] indication _____
- [ ] instrument _____
- [ ] instruction _____
- [ ] indifference _____
- [ ] intelligence _____

Check List

1. 想像力　　i ___imagination___ n
2. 印　象　　i _____ n
3. 改　善　　i _____ t
4. 獨　立　　i _____ e
5. 靈　感　　i _____ n

6. 免　疫　　i _____ y
7. 指　示　　i _____ n
8. 主　動　　i _____ e
9. 影　響　　i _____ t
10. 資　訊　　i _____ n

11. 監　禁　　i _____ t
12. 成　分　　i _____ t
13. 衝　動　　i _____ e
14. 事　件　　i _____ t
15. 智　力　　i _____ e

intensity 〔 ɪn'tɛnsətɪ 〕 *n.* 強烈

The *intensity* of Linda's love for music made her fly to Vienna to enter a music school. (學測 88, 90, 91 ②, 97 年,指考 93 ①, 96, 97 年)

intention 〔 ɪn'tɛnʃən 〕 *n.* 意圖

She went to Paris with the *intention* of learning French. (聯考 46, 71, 86 年,學測 86, 93, 98, 100 年,指考 91, 98, 101 年)

interval 〔'ɪntəvḷ 〕 *n.* 間隔

You had better have your car checked at regular *intervals*. (指考 94 年)

investigation 〔 ɪn͵vɛstə'geʃən 〕 *n.* 調查

The *investigation* of this case is still under way. It has not been finished. (聯考 48, 50, 55, 76 年,學測 98, 102 年,指考 92, 96, 98, 99, 101 年)

investment ﹝ ɪn'vɛstmənt ﹞ *n.* 投資

National bonds are a safe *investment*. (聯考 63,
69, 70, 71, 83, 87, 90 年，學測 91 ②, 98, 102 年，指考 96, 102 年)

irrigation ﹝ ˌɪrə'geʃən ﹞ *n.* 灌溉

Irrigation is needed to make crops grow in
dry regions. (聯考 73, 75 年)

issue ﹝ 'ɪʃu ﹞ *n.* 議題

The traffic problem is one of the main
issues facing our government. (聯考 55, 83, 85 年，
學測 83, 84, 85, 92 ②, 96, 98, 99, 102 年，指考 91, 93 ①, 94, 95, 98, 99, 101, 102 年)

J j

jewel ﹝ 'dʒuəl ﹞ *n.* 珠寶

Diamonds and precious stones are *jewels*.

(聯考 47, 56 年，學測 101 年，指考 97, 100 年)

L l

landmark〔'lænd,mɑrk〕*n.* 地標

The Shin-kong Mitsukoshi Tower is the *landmark* of Taipei. (模考 83 年，學測 93, 100 年)

landslide〔'lænd,slaɪd〕*n.* 山崩

Many houses were destroyed in the *landslide* after the typhoon. (聯考 89 年，學測 88, 93 年)

leisure〔'liʒɚ〕*n.* 空閒

Please drop in to see me at your *leisure*.

(聯考 68, 70, 90 年，指考 96 年)

literature〔'lɪtərətʃɚ〕*n.* 文學

Shakespeare is one of the most important figures in English *literature*. (聯考 54, 56, 68, 72, 87 年，

學測 91 ①②年，指考 99 年)

lottery〔'lɑtərɪ〕*n.* 彩券

He won a large sum of money in the *lottery*.

(聯考 86 年，學測 91 年)

luxury 〔'lʌkʃərɪ 〕 *n.* 奢侈品

His salary is so low that he can enjoy few
luxuries. (聯考 70 年，學測 92 ② 年)

M m

magnet 〔'mægnɪt 〕 *n.* 磁鐵

I use a *magnet* to hold notes on my
refrigerator. (模考 83 年)

medal 〔'mɛdḷ 〕 *n.* 獎牌

The athlete cherishes a hope of winning an
Olympic gold *medal*. (學測 83, 99 年)

memorial 〔 mə'mɔrɪəl 〕 *n.* 紀念碑

They erected a *memorial* in the park to
honor the great hero. (模考 91 年，聯考 51 年，學測 91 ① 年，
指考 97 年)

memory ('mɛmərɪ) *n.* 記憶
My grandmother is getting old and her
memory is failing. (模考 91 年，聯考 55, 62, 64, 65, 72, 74, 81, 88 年，學測 85, 92 ②, 97, 101 年，指考 93 ①, 97, 99 年)

mercy ('mɜsɪ) *n.* 慈悲
The warden showed no *mercy* to the
prisoners. (指考 93 ① 年)

mess (mɛs) *n.* 亂七八糟
After the party, the house was in a terrible
mess. (聯考 88 年)

message ('mɛsɪdʒ) *n.* 訊息
With e-mail, we can send *messages* to
people far away in a few seconds. (聯考 48, 49, 52, 75, 81, 82, 83, 84, 86, 88 年，學測 84, 91 ②, 92 ②, 94 年，指考 91, 94, 95, 100, 101 年)

miracle ('mɪrəkl̩) *n.* 奇蹟
It was a *miracle* that he should survive the
accident; the other passengers were all killed.
(聯考 88 年，學測 101 年)

misery (ˈmɪzərɪ) *n.* 不幸

Misery loves company. (聯考 53, 69 年，學測 102 年)

misunderstanding (ˌmɪsʌndəˈstændɪŋ)
n. 誤解

There must be some *misunderstanding.* I
meant 100 NTD, not 100 USD. (聯考 46, 67 年，

學測 91 ② 年)

modesty (ˈmɑdəstɪ) *n.* 謙虛

The young scientist showed great *modesty*
about his success. (聯考 50 年，學測 88 年)

moisture (ˈmɔɪstʃə) *n.* 濕氣

The desert air is so dry that it contains
hardly any *moisture*. (聯考 61 年，學測 100 年，指考 102 年)

moist	+ ture
|	|
潮濕的	+ *n.*

- ☐ mercy _____
- ☐ intensity _____
- ☐ modesty _____
- ☐ jewel _____
- ☐ medal _____

- ☐ misery _____
- ☐ intention _____
- ☐ luxury _____
- ☐ irrigation _____
- ☐ lottery _____

- ☐ memory _____
- ☐ leisure _____
- ☐ mess _____
- ☐ moisture _____
- ☐ issue _____

1. 山　崩　　l ___landslide___ e
2. 磁　鐵　　m _____ t
3. 奇　蹟　　m _____ e
4. 濕　氣　　m _____ e
5. 投　資　　i _____ t

6. 間　隔　　i _____ l
7. 調　查　　i _____ n
8. 謙　虛　　m _____ y
9. 訊　息　　m _____ e
10. 奢侈品　　l _____ y

11. 紀念碑　　m _____ l
12. 文　學　　l _____ e
13. 地　標　　l _____ k
14. 誤　解　　m _____ g
15. 議　題　　i _____ e

moral ('mɔrəl) *n.* 寓意

The *moral* of the movie was that scientists should respect the laws of nature. (聯考 60, 63, 67, 89, 90 年，學測 88, 98 年，指考 91 年)

motive ('motɪv) *n.* 動機

My only *motive* for writing this book is that the truth should be known. (聯考 61, 81 年，學測 91 ①, 92 ②, 98, 99 年，指考 93 ②, 94, 101 年)

movement ('muvmənt) *n.* 動作

The frog swallowed a fly with a swift *movement*. (聯考 58, 59, 68, 69, 74, 82, 83, 84, 90 年，學測 83, 84, 86, 89, 90, 91 ①, 92 ①②, 93, 94, 96, 98, 99, 100, 101 年，指考 91, 94, 97, 98, 99, 101, 102 年)

murmur ('mɝmɚ) *n.* 低語

There was a low *murmur* of conversation in the other room. (模考 82 年，學測 101 年，指考 94 年)

mystery ('mɪstrɪ) *n.* 神秘

No one knows why many airplanes disappeared in that area. It still remains a *mystery*. (聯考 50, 57, 81, 85, 90 年，學測 85, 86, 89 年，指考 95, 97 年)

N n

necessity 〔nə'sɛsətɪ〕 n. 需要

Necessity is the mother of invention. (聯考 46, 49, 51, 52, 53, 58, 65, 68, 72, 73, 78, 83, 88, 89 年，學測 85, 86, 91 ①②, 92 ①②, 97, 98, 99, 102 年，指考 91, 92, 93 ②, 98, 99, 100, 101, 102 年)

negotiation 〔nɪ͵goʃɪ'eʃən〕 n. 談判

Their conflict was settled by *negotiation*.

(聯考 85, 86 年，學測 90, 96 年，指考 101 年)

nickname 〔'nɪk͵nem〕 n. 綽號

He got the *nickname* "Four Eyes" because he wore glasses. (學測 99 年)

nonsense 〔'nɑnsɛns〕 n. 胡說八道

Don't believe what I say.
I'm just talking *nonsense*.

```
non + sense
 |      |
 no  + 意義
```

(聯考 69, 73, 87 年，學測 94 年)

nutrition 〔 nju'trɪʃən 〕 *n.* 營養

All living things need *nutrition* to grow
and stay healthy. (模考 82 年，聯考 87 年，學測 84, 88, 89,
92 ②, 98, 100 年，指考 101 年)

O o

obedience 〔 ə'bidɪəns 〕 *n.*
服從
Obedience is the number
one quality for a soldier.

(p.83～p.161)

(聯考 53, 60,69, 72, 75 年，學測 90, 92 ② 年，指考 97 年)

objective 〔 əb'dʒɛktɪv 〕 *n.* 目標

The main *objective* of this test is to find
out how much you have learned in high
school. (聯考 45, 50, 52, 61, 63, 65, 66, 69, 71, 72, 78, 87 年，學測 83, 84,
85, 90, 92 ①, 93, 94, 99, 101, 102 年，指考 92, 93 ①, 95, 97, 98, 99, 100, 102 年)

obligation 〔 ˌɑblə'geʃən 〕 *n.* 義務

Each adult man has a legal *obligation* to
serve in the army. (模考 91 年，聯考 61 年，指考 94 年)

obstacle 〔ˈɑbstəkḷ 〕 *n.* 障礙

He overcame the *obstacle* of blindness and became a musician. (聯考 71, 87 年，指考 95, 100 年)

occupation 〔ˌɑkjəˈpeʃən 〕 *n.* 職業

He is a merchant by *occupation*. (學測 97, 101 年，指考 94, 98 年)

organization 〔ˌɔrgənəˈzeʃən 〕 *n.* 組織

Mr. Lee donated regularly to a charity *organization*. (聯考 51, 62, 67, 68, 71, 83, 86, 88, 90 年，學測 92 ①, 96, 98, 99, 101 年，指考 91, 93 ①, 96, 97, 98, 101, 102 年)

origin 〔ˈɔrədʒɪn 〕 *n.* 起源

Some Japanese words are of Chinese *origin*. (模考 82 年，聯考 46, 53, 56, 72, 73, 79, 82, 87, 88, 89 年，學測 84, 85, 90, 91 ①②, 92 ①②, 93, 94, 97, 98, 99, 101, 102 年，指考 94, 96, 99, 100, 101, 102 年)

originality 〔 əˌrɪdʒəˈnæləti 〕 *n.* 創造力

The artist is famous for his genius and great *originality*. (學測 84, 97 年)

ornament ﹝ˈɔrnəmənt﹞ *n.* 裝飾品

The exotic *ornaments* I put in my room
were bought in Hawaii. (學測 90 年)

orphan ﹝ˈɔrfən﹞ *n.* 孤兒

An *orphan* is a child who has lost one or
both of its parents by death. (聯考 52 年)

outcome ﹝ˈaʊtˌkʌm﹞ *n.* 結果

On the basis of the clues, can you predict
the *outcome* of the story? (聯考 68, 86 年，學測 83, 100 年)

outlook ﹝ˈaʊtˌlʊk﹞ *n.* 看法

What is your *outlook* on this matter?

(聯考 63 年，學測 91 ②, 94 年)

P p

pace ﹝ pes ﹞ *n.* 步調

If we walk at this slow *pace*, we'll never
get to our destination on time. (聯考 60, 63 年，

學測 87 年，指考 91 年)

parade ﹝ pə'red ﹞ *n.* 遊行

The Olympic Games begin with a *parade* of all the competing nations. (學測 88 年)

paradox ﹝'pærə,dɑks ﹞ *n.* 矛盾

It's a *paradox*, but the older she gets the more active she becomes. (模考 83 年，學測 100 年)

passage ﹝'pæsɪdʒ ﹞ *n.* 通過

The bridge isn't strong enough to allow the *passage* of heavy trucks. (聯考 50, 53, 57, 72, 76, 77, 81, 82, 84, 85, 86, 87, 88, 89 年，學測 83, 84, 85, 86, 87, 88, 89, 90, 91 ②, 92 ①②, 93, 94, 96, 97, 99, 100, 101, 102 年，指考 91, 92, 93 ①②, 94, 95, 97, 98, 99, 100, 101, 102 年)

passion ﹝'pæʃən ﹞ *n.* 熱情

He delivered his lecture with great *passion*.

(聯考 64, 67, 88 年，學測 100 年，指考 96 年)

pastime ﹝'pæs,taɪm ﹞ *n.* 消遣

Kite flying has long been a favorite *pastime* of the Asian people. (聯考 68, 79, 87 年)

自 我 測 驗

- [ ] orphan　　　＿＿＿＿＿＿＿＿
- [ ] pace　　　　＿＿＿＿＿＿＿＿
- [ ] moral　　　＿＿＿＿＿＿＿＿
- [ ] passage　　＿＿＿＿＿＿＿＿
- [ ] origin　　　＿＿＿＿＿＿＿＿

- [ ] outcome　　＿＿＿＿＿＿＿＿
- [ ] parade　　　＿＿＿＿＿＿＿＿
- [ ] pastime　　＿＿＿＿＿＿＿＿
- [ ] motive　　　＿＿＿＿＿＿＿＿
- [ ] paradox　　＿＿＿＿＿＿＿＿

- [ ] objective　＿＿＿＿＿＿＿＿
- [ ] outlook　　＿＿＿＿＿＿＿＿
- [ ] passion　　＿＿＿＿＿＿＿＿
- [ ] ornament　＿＿＿＿＿＿＿＿
- [ ] obstacle　　＿＿＿＿＿＿＿＿

Check List

1. 裝飾品　　o ___*ornament*___ t

2. 職　業　　o _____ n

3. 創造力　　o _____ y

4. 義　務　　o _____ n

5. 營　養　　n _____ n

6. 胡說八道　n _____ e

7. 需　要　　n _____ y

8. 動　作　　m _____ t

9. 神　秘　　m _____ y

10. 低　語　　m _____ r

11. 談　判　　n _____ n

12. 組　織　　o _____ n

13. 服　從　　o _____ e

14. 綽　號　　n _____ e

15. 目　標　　o _____ e

penalty ('pɛnḷtɪ) *n.* 處罰

Penalties for traffic violations range from small fines to several years in jail. (指考 96 年)

perfection (pəˈfɛkʃən) *n.* 完美

The boss was demanding. He expected nothing but *perfection* from his employees.

(聯考 54, 59, 68, 69, 70, 71, 77, 82, 83, 85, 86, 89 年，學測 91 ①②, 92 ②, 97, 98 年，指考 91, 93 ②, 94, 95 年)

performance (pəˈfɔrməns) *n.* 表演

The final *performance* of the play will take place on Monday. (聯考 48, 49, 50, 51, 62, 63, 65, 66, 70, 81, 85, 86, 87, 88, 90 年，學測 83, 91 ①, 92 ①, 93, 94, 97, 99, 100, 101 年，指考 92, 93 ①, 95, 96, 97, 99, 100, 101 年)

permission (pəˈmɪʃən) *n.* 允許

You can't enter that room without *permission*. (模考 91 年，聯考 51, 59, 81, 84, 90 年，學測 83, 96 年，指考 91, 94, 98 年)

perseverance 〔͵pɝsə'vɪrəns 〕*n.* 毅力

The road to success lies through ability and *perseverance.* (聯考 48, 51, 67 年，指考 94 年)

perspiration 〔͵pɝspə'reʃən 〕*n.* 流汗

Genius is one percent inspiration and ninety-nine percent *perspiration.* (指考 91 年)

per	+	spir	+ ation
|		|	|
through	+	*breathe* +	*n.* (透過皮膚呼吸)

phenomenon 〔 fə'namə͵nan 〕*n.* 現象

The inflation is an economic *phenomenon* worthy of note. (聯考 50 年，學測 84, 91 ①, 100 年，指考 93 ②, 96, 101 年)

philosophy 〔 fə'lasəfɪ 〕*n.* 哲學

"There's no such thing as a free lunch" is his father's *philosophy.* (聯考 51, 70, 87 年，指考 100, 101 年)

pioneer 〔͵paɪəˋnɪr〕 *n.* 先驅

Dr. Peterson is a *pioneer* in modern medical science. (指考 94 年)

policy 〔ˋpɑləsɪ〕 *n.* 政策

It has always been the *policy* of this company to promote existing staff to senior positions. (聯考 66, 67 年，學測 91 ② 年，指考 93 ②, 94, 96 年)

portrait 〔ˋportret〕 *n.* 肖像

Above his desk hung a *portrait* of his wife, which was painted by a famous artist.

(模考 83 年，學測 101 年)

potential 〔pəˋtɛnʃəl〕 *n.* 潛力

She has an ear for music; in other words, she has great *potential* in music. (模考 82 年，

聯考 85, 90 年，學測 87, 96, 99, 100 年，指考 92, 93 ① ②, 94, 97, 100, 101, 102 年)

precaution (prɪˈkɔʃən) *n.* 預防措施

It is mandatory for us to take *precautions* against typhoons. (指考 92 年)

preference (ˈprɛfərəns) *n.* 偏愛

People with a *preference* for fat-rich foods run a high risk of heart disease. (模考 91 年，聯考 48, 59, 61, 68, 76, 77, 80, 87, 89, 90 年，學測 84, 93, 98, 101, 102 年，指考 99, 100, 101 年)

prescription (prɪˈskrɪpʃən) *n.* 藥方

Before writing a *prescription*, the doctor has to diagnose your disease. (模考 83 年，聯考 55, 74, 87 年，學測 86, 94 年，指考 96 年)

pre	+ script	+ ion
before	+ *write*	+ *n.*

pressure (ˈprɛʃɚ) *n.* 壓力

Many students are under great *pressure* to achieve excellent academic performance.

(模考 82 年，聯考 76, 81, 86 年，學測 93, 99 年，指考 91, 93 ①, 97, 101, 102 年)

principle 〔ˈprɪnsəpḷ〕 *n.* 原則

One *principle* in my family is no television during mealtimes. (聯考 60 年)

priority 〔praɪˈɔrətɪ〕 *n.* 優先的事物

As a father, my top *priority* is to take care of my family. (模考 91 年，聯考 71 年，學測 94 年，指考 92, 93②年)

privacy 〔ˈpraɪvəsɪ〕 *n.* 隱私

Though my father is very strict with me, he seldom invades my *privacy*. (模考 82, 91 年，聯考 80 年，指考 92, 96, 100 年)

privilege 〔ˈprɪvḷɪdʒ〕 *n.* 特權

Only members have the *privilege* of using the sports facilities. (模考 82, 91 年，聯考 68 年，學測 88, 97 年，指考 100 年)

procedure 〔 prə'sidʒə 〕 *n.* 程序

You have to follow the regular *procedure* to apply for the license. (聯考 90 年，學測 85 年，指考 97, 101 年)

pro	+ ced	+ ure
|	|	|
forward	+ *go*	+ *n.*

pro	+ cess
|	|
forward	+ *go*

process 〔'prɑsɛs 〕 *n.* 過程

During the *process* of growth, we inevitably meet with some challenges. (聯考 70, 78, 81, 87, 88, 89 年，學測 83, 84, 88, 91 ①, 97, 98, 99, 100, 102 年，指考 93 ①②, 95, 96, 98, 99, 101, 102 年)

profession 〔 prə'fɛʃən 〕 *n.* 職業

Mr. Smith sometimes writes novels, but he is a physician by *profession*. (聯考 58, 80, 82 年，學測 92 ②, 100 年，指考 96, 97 年)

proportion 〔 prə'porʃən 〕 *n.* 比例

Nowadays advertising costs are no longer in reasonable *proportion* to the total cost of the product. (聯考 88 年，指考 93 ① 年)

- [ ] process　　　　＿＿＿＿＿＿＿＿
- [ ] performance　　＿＿＿＿＿＿＿＿
- [ ] pioneer　　　　＿＿＿＿＿＿＿＿
- [ ] priority　　　　＿＿＿＿＿＿＿＿
- [ ] pressure　　　　＿＿＿＿＿＿＿＿

- [ ] portrait　　　　＿＿＿＿＿＿＿＿
- [ ] phenomenon　　＿＿＿＿＿＿＿＿
- [ ] permission　　　＿＿＿＿＿＿＿＿
- [ ] principle　　　　＿＿＿＿＿＿＿＿
- [ ] proportion　　　＿＿＿＿＿＿＿＿

- [ ] policy　　　　　＿＿＿＿＿＿＿＿
- [ ] profession　　　＿＿＿＿＿＿＿＿
- [ ] prescription　　＿＿＿＿＿＿＿＿
- [ ] privacy　　　　　＿＿＿＿＿＿＿＿
- [ ] precaution　　　＿＿＿＿＿＿＿＿

Check List

1. 毅　力　　　p _perseverance_ e
2. 處　罰　　　p ＿＿＿＿＿＿＿＿＿＿ y
3. 預防措施　　p ＿＿＿＿＿＿＿＿＿＿ n
4. 特　權　　　p ＿＿＿＿＿＿＿＿＿＿ e
5. 完　美　　　p ＿＿＿＿＿＿＿＿＿＿ n

6. 現　象　　　p ＿＿＿＿＿＿＿＿＿＿ n
7. 職　業　　　p ＿＿＿＿＿＿＿＿＿＿ n
8. 程　序　　　p ＿＿＿＿＿＿＿＿＿＿ e
9. 藥　方　　　p ＿＿＿＿＿＿＿＿＿＿ n
10. 偏　愛　　　p ＿＿＿＿＿＿＿＿＿＿ e

11. 潛　力　　　p ＿＿＿＿＿＿＿＿＿＿ l
12. 流　汗　　　p ＿＿＿＿＿＿＿＿＿＿ n
13. 原　則　　　p ＿＿＿＿＿＿＿＿＿＿ e
14. 隱　私　　　p ＿＿＿＿＿＿＿＿＿＿ y
15. 哲　學　　　p ＿＿＿＿＿＿＿＿＿＿ y

proposal ﹝ prə'pozḷ ﹞ *n.* 提議

His *proposal* was rejected because it was considered impractical. (聯考 63, 66, 67, 68, 71, 88 年，

學測 84, 86, 87, 88, 91 ①, 92 ②, 100, 102 年，指考 93 ②, 94, 98, 101 年)

$$\begin{array}{ccc}
\text{pro} & +\text{pos} & +\text{al} \\
| & | & | \\
\textit{forward} & +\textit{put} & +\textit{n.}
\end{array}$$

protest ﹝'protɛst ﹞ *n.* 抗議

The manager resigned in *protest* against the company's new regulation. (聯考 50, 59 年，

學測 91 ①, 101 年，指考 91, 97, 98 年)

proverb ﹝'prɑvɝb ﹞ *n.* 諺語

Proverbs are popular sayings that stand the test of time. (聯考 85 年，學測 91 ② 年，指考 91, 99 年)

puzzle ﹝'pʌzḷ ﹞ *n.* 謎

Our family puts a jigsaw *puzzle* together every Christmas. (聯考 50, 51, 52, 62 年，指考 100 年)

Q q

qualification 〔ˌkwɑləfəˈkeʃən 〕 *n.* 資格

What are the important *qualifications* of a good teacher? (聯考 52, 66, 72, 73, 74, 75, 86 年，學測 88 年，指考 92, 93 ②, 94, 97, 98 年)

quality 〔ˈkwɑlətɪ 〕 *n.* 特質

Courage is one of the *qualities* of a good soldier. (聯考 46, 63, 67, 68, 69, 70, 74, 84 年，學測 89, 91 ②, 93, 96, 97, 98, 100, 102 年，指考 91, 92, 93 ②, 95, 98, 99 年)

quantity 〔ˈkwɑntətɪ 〕 *n.* 數量

To irrigate the field, the farmer used a large *quantity* of water. (學測 85, 90, 102 年)

quarrel 〔ˈkwɔrəl 〕 *n.* 爭論

I had a *quarrel* with him last night and we were both angry. (聯考 46, 60, 62, 65, 86 年)

R r

range 〔 rendʒ 〕 *n.* 範圍

Be sure that the game you select is within the *range* of your students' ability. (聯考 52, 78,

90 年，學測 91 ②, 92 ②, 96, 101 年，指考 93 ①, 95, 100, 102 年)

recession 〔 rɪ'sɛʃən 〕 *n.* 衰退

Unemployment rate is
high because the
economy is in *recession*.

re	+ cess	+ ion
back	+ *go*	+ *n.*

(聯考 83 年，指考 92, 93 ②, 98, 99 年)

recipient 〔 rɪ'sɪpɪənt 〕 *n.* 接受者

The *recipient* of the heart transplant is a
five-year-old boy. (模考 91 年，學測 83 年)

recognition 〔ˌrɛkəg'nɪʃən 〕 *n.* 認可

After a series of successful movies, Jackie
Chan finally won worldwide *recognition*.

(模考 91 年，聯考 48, 67, 68, 72, 73, 81, 84, 85, 88, 90 年，學測 85, 88, 91 ①,

92 ①, 93, 96, 97, 101, 102 年，指考 91, 93 ①②, 96, 99 年)

recreation (ˌrɛkrɪˈeʃən) *n.* 消遣

Reading and walking are his favorite kinds of *recreation*. (聯考 54, 73, 78, 84 年,學測 96 年)

reference (ˈrɛfərəns) *n.* 參考

If you have any question, you can consult the *reference* book. (聯考 58, 62, 63, 69, 88, 89 年,學測 87, 92 ②, 93, 98, 99, 100, 102 年,指考 91, 92, 93 ①, 95, 97, 98, 99, 100, 101, 102 年)

reflection (rɪˈflɛkʃən) *n.* 反射

The *reflection* of the trees in the water was quite clear. (模考 91 年,聯考 48, 52, 81, 82, 86, 87, 89 年,學測 83 年,指考 91, 93 ①②, 97, 101 年)

re	+ flect	+ ion
back	+ *bend*	+ *n.*

reform (rɪˈfɔrm) *n.* 改革

Our society is pressing for an immediate *reform* to change the status quo. (模考 91 年,聯考 50, 85 年,學測 94 年,指考 98, 100 年)

region 〔'ridʒən 〕 *n.* 地區

The desert *region* is sparsely populated.

(聯考 51, 58, 65, 75 年，學測 88, 89, 98, 99 年，指考 93 ②, 96, 97, 99 年)

remedy 〔'rɛmədɪ 〕 *n.* 治療法

Love is the best *remedy* for hatred.   (指考 95, 97 年)

reputation 〔,rɛpjə'teʃən 〕 *n.* 名聲

He enjoys a good *reputation* as a scholar.

(模考 91 年，聯考 45, 85 年，學測 90, 91 ②, 94 年，指考 93 ②, 101 年)

request 〔 rɪ'kwɛst 〕 *n.* 要求

The pianist played one more song at the
request of the audience.   (聯考 48, 49, 62, 63, 64, 79, 80, 82,

89 年，學測 90, 92 ②, 96, 98, 101 年，指考 93 ①, 99, 100 年)

reservation 〔,rɛzə'veʃən 〕 *n.* 預訂

I have already made all the *reservations*
for this trip.   (聯考 57, 60, 67, 71, 81, 83, 88 年，學測 83, 91 ②, 92 ①,

93, 102 年，指考 93 ②, 94, 98, 99 年)

resident〔'rɛzədənt 〕 *n.* 居民

There are many foreign *residents* living in this neighborhood. （聯考 66, 73, 85, 87 年，指考 93 ①②, 98 年）

resistance〔 rɪ'zɪstəns 〕 *n.* 抵抗

A reduction in the number of white blood cells lowers *resistance* to disease. （聯考 56, 63, 66, 68, 69, 71, 83, 87 年，學測 87, 91 ①, 92 ①, 94, 99, 100, 102 年，指考 96, 98, 101 年）

re	+ sist	+ ance
back	+ *stand*	+ *n.*

resolution〔ˌrɛzə'luʃən 〕 *n.* 決心

A person who hesitates a lot cannot make *resolutions* even about trivial matters.

（模考 90 年，聯考 90 年，學測 98 年，指考 101 年）

resort〔 rɪ'zɔrt 〕 *n.* 勝地

On holidays, every *resort* is crowded with holiday-makers. （學測 88 年，指考 93, 94, 96, 101 年）

自我測驗

- [ ] reform   _____
- [ ] remedy   _____
- [ ] resort   _____
- [ ] range   _____
- [ ] puzzle   _____

- [ ] request   _____
- [ ] quarrel   _____
- [ ] region   _____
- [ ] recipient   _____
- [ ] quality   _____

- [ ] resolution   _____
- [ ] proposal   _____
- [ ] recognition _____
- [ ] resident   _____
- [ ] reference   _____

Check List

1. 決　心　r＿＿＿＿ *resolution* ＿＿＿＿ n

2. 反　射　r＿＿＿＿＿＿＿＿＿＿ n

3. 抵　抗　r＿＿＿＿＿＿＿＿＿＿ e

4. 消　遣　r＿＿＿＿＿＿＿＿＿＿ n

5. 預　訂　r＿＿＿＿＿＿＿＿＿＿ n

6. 提　議　p＿＿＿＿＿＿＿＿＿＿ l

7. 資　格　q＿＿＿＿＿＿＿＿＿＿ n

8. 數　量　q＿＿＿＿＿＿＿＿＿＿ y

9. 爭　論　q＿＿＿＿＿＿＿＿＿＿ l

10. 諺　語　p＿＿＿＿＿＿＿＿＿＿ b

11. 抗　議　p＿＿＿＿＿＿＿＿＿＿ t

12. 特　質　q＿＿＿＿＿＿＿＿＿＿ y

13. 衰　退　r＿＿＿＿＿＿＿＿＿＿ n

14. 名　聲　r＿＿＿＿＿＿＿＿＿＿ n

15. 參　考　r＿＿＿＿＿＿＿＿＿＿ e

revenge 〔 rɪ'vɛndʒ 〕 *n.* 報復

Jean decided to take *revenge* on Henry for hurting her feelings. (模考 82 年，聯考 69 年，學測 91 ①年)

reward 〔 rɪ'wɔrd 〕 *n.* 酬勞

I received a *reward* for looking after the children during her absence. (聯考 54, 57, 87, 88, 89 年，學測 83, 87, 92 ②, 96, 99 年，指考 92, 98, 99 年)

rival 〔 'raɪvḷ 〕 *n.* 對手

Shakespeare has no *rival* in the depth of his influence on English. (聯考 60, 62, 66 年，學測 98 年)

rumor 〔 'rumɚ 〕 *n.* 謠言

Rumor has it that the official took a bribe.

(聯考 64 年，學測 92 ②, 101 年)

S s

sacrifice 〔 'sækrə,faɪs 〕 *n.* 犧牲

Parents often make *sacrifices* for their children. (聯考 68 年，指考 92, 101 年)

sake 〔 sek 〕 *n.* 緣故

The couple stayed together for the *sake* of the children. (指考 96 年)

scandal 〔'skænd!〕 *n.* 醜聞

When a public official is found involved in a *scandal*, he usually has to resign. (聯考 82 年，學測 92 ② 年，指考 92, 95 年)

scenery 〔'sinərɪ〕 *n.* 景色

The beautiful *scenery* in the country may refresh you. (聯考 48, 90 年，學測 88, 97 年，指考 93 ①, 94 年)

security 〔 sɪ'kjurətɪ 〕 *n.* 安全

Children count on their parents for love and *security*. (學測 86, 92 ②, 94, 98 年，指考 92, 97, 98, 100, 101, 102 年)

setback 〔'sɛt,bæk〕 *n.* 挫折

The outcome of the election was a major *setback* for the ruling party. (聯考 68 年)

settler (ˈsɛtlɚ) *n.* 殖民者

The first white *settlers* in South Africa were Dutch. (指考 95 年)

shadow (ˈʃædo) *n.* 影子

The setting sun made the *shadows* longer and larger.

shelter (ˈʃɛltɚ) *n.* 避難所

The big tree was a good *shelter* from the rain. (聯考 81, 87 年，指考 91, 102 年)

signal (ˈsɪgnḷ) *n.* 信號

Signals are made by day with flags and by night with lights. (聯考 64, 81, 82, 83, 85, 90 年，學測 88, 92 ②，93 年，指考 92, 95 年)

signature (ˈsɪgnətʃɚ) *n.* 簽名

He put his *signature* on the contract. (模考 91 年，聯考 47, 82 年，學測 91 ②年)

situation 〔,sɪtʃu'eʃən 〕 *n.* 情況

He found himself in a difficult *situation*
financially. (聯考 51, 63, 65, 67, 86, 87, 89 年，學測 83, 84, 86, 88, 91 ①,
92 ②, 98, 100, 101 年，指考 91, 97, 98, 101 年)

sorrow 〔'saro 〕 *n.* 悲傷

To the *sorrow* of all those who were present,
Mr. Smith died. (聯考 48, 67, 69, 89 年，學測 87, 89, 99, 101 年，
指考 91, 97, 98 年)

span 〔 spæn 〕 *n.* 期間

Our minds like to wander. Our attention
spans are short. (聯考 67 年，指考 95 年)

spectator 〔'spɛktetɚ 〕 *n.* 觀衆

Over 5000 *spectators* went to the soccer
game. (學測 88 年，指考 97 年)

spect	+ at(e)	+ or
see	+ *v.*	+ 人

spirit ('spɪrɪt) *n.* 精神

The *spirit* is willing but the flesh is weak.

(聯考 67, 68, 70, 82, 84, 85 年，學測 90, 93, 94, 96, 101 年，指考 93 ①, 95, 102 年)

splendor ('splɛndə) *n.* 光輝

We are attracted to the *splendor* of the sunset.

(聯考 51 年)

spot (spɑt) *n.* 斑點

The leopard cannot change its *spots*. (聯考 53,

84, 85 年，學測 84, 88, 90, 96 年)

statesman ('stetsmən) *n.* 政治家

Churchill is considered to be the greatest
statesman of modern England. (聯考 51, 64 年)

status ('stetəs) *n.* 地位

Membership in a gym or health club is still a
status symbol. (聯考 76 年，學測 100, 101, 102 年，指考 98, 100 年)

stimulation 〔͵stɪmjə'leʃən 〕 *n.* 刺激

Successful people often need more challenge and *stimulation* than others.

(聯考 88 年，指考 97, 101 年)

strength 〔 strɛŋθ 〕 *n.* 力量

He is too small; he doesn't have the *strength* to lift that rock. (聯考 48, 49, 61, 66, 69, 74, 75, 83,

86 年，學測 84, 92 ②, 93, 98 年，指考 92, 93 ②, 97, 98, 100 年)

suicide 〔'suə͵saɪd 〕 *n.* 自殺

That man committed *suicide*; that is to say, he killed himself. (聯考 53 年，

學測 92 ①年，指考 100 年)

sui	+	cide
self	+	*kill*

surgeon 〔'sɝdʒən 〕 *n.* 外科醫生

He is the best *surgeon* in town to operate on a case like this. (聯考 49, 60 年，指考 91 年)

☐ splendor _____

☐ scandal _____

☐ stimulation _____

☐ signal _____

☐ sake _____

☐ statesman _____

☐ rumor _____

☐ span _____

☐ rival _____

☐ revenge _____

☐ shelter _____

☐ setback _____

☐ reward _____

☐ surgeon _____

☐ settler _____

Check List

1. 悲　　傷　　s ___*sorrow*___ w
2. 力　　量　　s _____ h
3. 斑　　點　　s _____ t
4. 地　　位　　s _____ s
5. 自　　殺　　s _____ e

6. 犧　　牲　　s _____ e
7. 殖民者　　s _____ r
8. 醜　　聞　　s _____ l
9. 影　　子　　s _____ w
10. 景　　色　　s _____ y

11. 情　　況　　s _____ n
12. 安　　全　　s _____ y
13. 簽　　名　　s _____ e
14. 觀　　衆　　s _____ r
15. 精　　神　　s _____ t

surgery ﹝'sɜdʒərɪ﹞ *n.* 手術

You can have plastic *surgery* instead of going on a diet. (學測 93, 97 年，指考 93 ②, 102 年)

surroundings ﹝sə'raʊndɪŋz﹞ *n. pl.* 環境

I'd like to bring up my child in healthy *surroundings*. (聯考 47, 53, 69, 71 年，學測 91 ① 年，指考 94 年)

survey ﹝'sɜve﹞ *n.* 調查

We are interested in the results of your recent *survey*. (學測 91 ②, 92 ① 年，指考 92, 93 ②, 98 年)

suspect ﹝'sʌspɛkt﹞ *n.* 嫌疑犯

The *suspect* turned himself in to the police four hours later. (聯考 59, 61, 64 年，學測 97, 102 年，指考 96 年)

suspense ﹝sə'spɛns﹞ *n.* 懸疑

Tell me what happened at the end of the game. Don't keep me in *suspense*. (模考 83 年，聯考 81 年)

suspicion 〔 səˈspɪʃən 〕 *n.* 懷疑

His behavior aroused my *suspicion*. (模考 91 年，

聯考 48, 72, 86, 89 年，學測 100 年，指考 94, 102 年)

sympathy 〔ˈsɪmpəθɪ 〕 *n.* 同情

Out of *sympathy* for the homeless children, he gave them shelter for the night. (模考 89 年，

聯考 48, 49, 63, 81, 82, 85, 86, 89 年，

學測 83, 99 年，指考 96, 98, 99, 100 年)

sym	+ pathy
same	+ *feeling*

system 〔ˈsɪstəm 〕 *n.* 制度

Our company has already adopted the five-day work week *system*. (聯考 81, 82, 87, 88, 89, 90 年，

學測 91 ②, 94, 96, 98, 100, 101 年，指考 92, 93 ①②, 94, 95, 97, 98, 100, 101, 102 年)

T t

tag 〔 tæg 〕 *n.* 標籤

Each coat in the store had a *tag* with the price on it.

tailor (ˈtelɚ) *n.* 裁縫師

Mr. Smith always has his suits made by a
tailor. (聯考 48, 68, 69 年，學測 101 年)

technique (tɛkˈnik) *n.* 技巧

Do you know the *techniques* of film-making?

(聯考 69, 90 年，學測 99, 101 年，指考 93 ①②, 97, 101, 102 年)

temptation (tɛmpˈteʃən) *n.* 誘惑

A scholar should not give in to the *temptation*
to be lazy. (聯考 49, 82, 83 年，學測 94 年，指考 99 年)

tension (ˈtɛnʃən) *n.* 緊張

You could feel the *tension* when the two
rivals walked into the room. (聯考 46, 51, 63, 77, 82 年，

學測 86 年，指考 100, 101 年)

theory (ˈθiərɪ) *n.* 理論

Your plan is practicable in *theory*, but not
practical enough. (聯考 50, 63, 64, 65 年，學測 93, 98 年，

指考 94, 95 年)

track 〔 træk 〕 *n.* 蹤跡

I have lost *track* of some of my classmates since I left school. (聯考 68, 88 年，指考 96 年)

trait 〔 tret 〕 *n.* 特性

Her generosity is one of her most pleasing *traits*. (聯考 79 年，學測 99 年，指考 101 年)

transportation 〔ˌtrænspəˈteʃən 〕 *n.* 交通工具

To avoid being caught in a traffic jam, you had better take public *transportation*. (聯考 52, 53, 70, 80, 81, 82, 87 年，學測 88, 90, 97, 98 年，指考 92, 93 ②, 94 年)

trans	+ port	+ ation
|	|	|
across	+ *carry* +	*n.*

treatment 〔ˈtritmənt 〕 *n.* 治療

She was under medical *treatment* for her skin disease. (聯考 59, 62, 84, 88, 90 年，學測 83, 86, 87, 88, 89, 92 ①②, 93, 96, 97, 100, 101 年，指考 91, 95, 98, 102 年)

V v

variety 〔vəˈraɪətɪ〕 *n.* 多樣性

This library has a wide *variety* of books.
You can find books on any topic you are
interested in. (聯考 54, 63, 79, 87, 90 年，學測 86, 89, 92 ②, 98,
100, 101 年，指考 92, 93 ①②, 95, 97, 99 年)

victim 〔ˈvɪktɪm〕 *n.* 受害者

A fund was opened to help the *victims* of
the flood. (聯考 68, 69 年，學測 86, 90, 92 ② 年，指考 91, 98, 100 年)

visibility 〔ˌvɪzəˈbɪlətɪ〕 *n.* 能見度

In the fog, the *visibility* is very poor. (學測 89,
90 年，指考 96 年)

volume 〔ˈvɑljəm〕 *n.* 音量

Please turn down the *volume* of the radio.
It's too loud. (指考 95 年)

W w

whistle 〔ˈhwɪsḷ〕 *n.* 哨子

The policeman blew his *whistle* as the thief ran away.

wrinkle 〔ˈrɪŋkḷ〕 *n.* 皺紋

Her face was old and covered in *wrinkles*.

(模考 83 年，學測 91 ①, 98 年)

---【 劉毅老師的話 】---

孩子們，背單字是成功的第一步，目前你已經背了本書 374 個名詞。好的開始是成功的一半，繼續努力，你的目標已向前邁進了一大步。

自 我 測 驗

- [ ] tag　　　　　　_____
- [ ] temptation　　　_____
- [ ] visibility　　　_____
- [ ] survey　　　　　_____
- [ ] track　　　　　　_____

- [ ] tailor　　　　　_____
- [ ] suspicion　　　_____
- [ ] victim　　　　　_____
- [ ] wrinkle　　　　_____
- [ ] suspect　　　　_____

- [ ] tension　　　　_____
- [ ] trait　　　　　_____
- [ ] system　　　　_____
- [ ] surgery　　　　_____
- [ ] whistle　　　　_____

Check List

1. 治　療　　t ___treatment___ t
2. 多樣性　　v _____ y
3. 技　巧　　t _____ e
4. 交通工具　t _____ n
5. 能見度　　v _____ y

6. 環　境　　s _____ s
7. 懷　疑　　s _____ n
8. 理　論　　t _____ y
9. 懸　疑　　s _____ e
10. 誘　惑　　t _____ n

11. 同　情　　s _____ y
12. 音　量　　v _____ e
13. 受害者　　v _____ m
14. 嫌疑犯　　s _____ t
15. 手　術　　s _____ y

★ 動 詞 ★

abide 〔 ə'baɪd 〕 v. 遵守

Once you make a promise, you should always *abide* by it.

abolish 〔 ə'balɪʃ 〕 v. 廢除

We have to *abolish* the old system before adopting the new one. (聯考 49 年，指考 98, 102 年)

absorb 〔 əb'sɔrb 〕 v. 吸收

Anything black *absorbs* most of the light rays that fall on it. (聯考 47, 66, 69, 73 年，學測 99, 100 年，指考 99 年)

abuse 〔 ə'bjuz 〕 v. 虐待

In the story, Cinderella was *abused* by her step-mother.

(聯考 66, 83, 86 年，學測 101 年，指考 97, 102 年)

```
ab + use
 |     |
not + use
```

accommodate〔əˋkɑməˏdet〕v. 容納

I think the hall is big enough to *accommodate* 200 people. (聯考 67, 89 年，指考 96 年)

accuse〔əˋkjuz〕v. 控告

He was *accused* of robbing the bank, but actually he had nothing to do with the robbery. (模考 91 年，聯考 61, 67, 85 年，學測 88 年，指考 95 年)

achieve〔əˋtʃiv〕v. 達成

Work hard, and you will *achieve* your goal.

(聯考 50, 65, 67, 68, 69, 70, 71, 73, 74, 85, 87, 88, 90 年，學測 85, 87, 88, 91 ①, 92 ②, 93, 98 年，指考 92, 93 ①, 97, 102 年)

acknowledge〔əkˋnɑlɪdʒ〕v. 承認

He *acknowledged* that he was defeated.

(模考 91 年，聯考 55, 68, 90 年，指考 97 年)

acquaint〔əˋkwent〕v. 使熟悉

The professor did his best to *acquaint* the students with new ideas. (聯考 49, 55, 61, 66, 67, 68, 84 年)

acquire 〔 əˈkwaɪr 〕 v. 獲得

He *acquired* great wealth by investing in real property. (模考 91 年,聯考 54, 60, 86 年,學測 101 年,指考 95, 100 年)

adapt 〔 əˈdæpt 〕 v. 使適應

When you go to a new country, you must *adapt* yourself to new manners and customs.

(模考 82 年,聯考 81, 89 年,學測 88, 96, 98 年,指考 94, 96, 98 年)

```
ad + apt
 |     |
to  + fit
```

adjust 〔 əˈdʒʌst 〕 v. 調整

There is a problem at our television station. Please don't *adjust* your set. (聯考 64, 78, 89 年,學測 90, 94, 96, 99 年,指考 94, 97, 100 年)

admire 〔 ədˈmaɪr 〕 v. 欽佩

Of all my friends, Percy is the one I *admire* most. (聯考 47, 68, 74, 79, 87, 88 年,學測 91 ②, 92 ①, 93, 94 年)

admit〔əd'mɪt〕 *v.* 承認

Peter *admitted* that he had made a serious
mistake. (聯考 47, 64, 66, 70, 73, 81, 87 年，學測 90, 91 ①②, 96, 101 年，
指考 93 ①②, 94, 99, 102 年)

adopt〔ə'dɑpt〕*v.* 採用

After careful discussion, we decided to
adopt plan B. (模考 82 年，聯考 49, 75, 81 年，學測 83, 88,
97, 98, 101 年，指考 93 ①, 95, 98, 100, 102 年)

afford〔ə'ford〕*v.* 負擔得起

We are so busy that we can't *afford* to have
a nice lie-in even on Sunday morning.

(聯考 45, 49, 54, 66, 68, 76, 87, 90 年，學測 86, 96 年，指考 93 ①, 94 年)

amend〔ə'mɛnd〕*v.* 修正

It is high time the government *amended*
the law.

analyze〔ˈænḷˌaɪz〕 v. 分析

Faced with a problem, you have to *analyze* it first, and then try to find a solution.

(聯考 85, 90 年，學測 88, 87, 96 年，指考 93 ②, 100 年)

announce〔əˈnaʊns〕 v. 宣布

It has been officially *announced* that he will not run for reelection.   (聯考 55, 66, 73, 77 年，學測 83, 88, 92 ①, 100 年，指考 93 ②, 94, 97, 102 年)

anticipate〔ænˈtɪsəˌpet〕 v. 預期

As you know, when college students *anticipate* their future employment, they often think of status and income.   (聯考 66 年，學測 92 ② 年)

apologize〔əˈpɑləˌdʒaɪz〕 v. 道歉

The boy *apologized* to the teacher for his improper behavior.   (聯考 49, 68, 75 年，學測 85, 88, 96 年，指考 92, 94, 97 年)

appeal 〔ə'pil〕v. 吸引

The old principal's address *appealed* strongly to the students. (模考 82 年，聯考 46, 51, 69, 77, 88, 90 年，學測 84, 85, 86, 97, 99, 100, 101 年，指考 99, 101 年)

applaud 〔ə'plɔd〕v. 鼓掌

When the pianist finished playing, the audience *applauded* loudly. (聯考 64, 73 年)

appreciate 〔ə'priʃɪ,et〕v. 感激

I really *appreciate* what you did for all of us. (聯考 56, 58, 62, 67, 72, 79, 84, 85, 86, 87, 88 年，學測 93 年，指考 91, 92, 93 ②, 95, 96, 98, 99, 100 年)

approach 〔ə'protʃ〕v. 接近

Many students find it hard to focus on their studies when holidays are *approaching*.

(模考 91 年，聯考 48, 50, 59, 64, 65, 66, 79 年，學測 85, 88, 91 ①, 92 ①, 98, 99, 102 年，指考 91, 95, 99 年)

自 我 測 驗

- [ ] abuse　　　　　_____
- [ ] admit　　　　　_____
- [ ] afford　　　　　_____
- [ ] appeal　　　　　_____
- [ ] accuse　　　　　_____

- [ ] amend　　　　　_____
- [ ] achieve　　　　_____
- [ ] adjust　　　　　_____
- [ ] acquire　　　　_____
- [ ] admire　　　　　_____

- [ ] approach　　　_____
- [ ] adapt　　　　　_____
- [ ] adopt　　　　　_____
- [ ] acquaint　　　_____
- [ ] absorb　　　　_____

Check List

1. 廢　除　　a ___abolish___ h
2. 鼓　掌　　a _____ d
3. 使熟悉　　a _____ t
4. 道　歉　　a _____ e
5. 容　納　　a _____ e

6. 感　激　　a _____ e
7. 承　認　　a _____ e
8. 欽　佩　　a _____ e
9. 預　期　　a _____ e
10. 控　告　　a _____ e

11. 承　認　　a _____ t
12. 分　析　　a _____ e
13. 吸　收　　a _____ b
14. 宣　布　　a _____ e
15. 遵　守　　a _____ e

approve 〔ə'pruv〕 v. 贊成

He does not *approve* of the plan. (聯考 49, 50, 54, 69, 73 年，指考 93 ①②, 97, 99, 100, 102 年)

argue 〔'ɑrgjʊ〕 v. 爭論

I don't think it's of any use *arguing* with him. (聯考 45, 46, 51, 54, 59, 61, 62, 63, 67, 72, 78, 79, 88 年，學測 87, 91 ①②, 92 ①②年，指考 92, 95, 102 年)

arise 〔ə'raɪz〕 v. 發生

Many problems *arise* from the use of credit cards. (聯考 53, 63 年，學測 94, 99 年，指考 94, 97, 99 年)

assemble 〔ə'sɛmbḷ〕 v. 裝配

He can *assemble* a bicycle if he is given all the parts. (聯考 63, 85 年，學測 87, 92 ②, 102 年，指考 94 年)

assign 〔ə'saɪn〕 v. 指派

as + sign
to + 簽名

Sarah was *assigned* by the manager to do the research and make a report. (聯考 52, 74, 87 年，學測 102 年，指考 93 ①, 98 年)

associate 〔 ə'soʃɪ͵et 〕 *v.* 聯想

We naturally *associate* the name of Darwin with the doctrine of evolution. (模考 91 年，聯考 54, 69, 74, 89 年，學測 85, 97, 101 年，指考 91, 93 ②, 94, 95, 98, 99, 100, 101, 102 年)

assume 〔 ə'sjum 〕 *v.* 擔任

It is reported that the new mayor will *assume* office on August 15. (聯考 74 年，學測 101 年，指考 101 年)

assure 〔 ə'ʃur 〕 *v.* 保證

I *assure* you that this medicine doesn't have any side effects.

(聯考 70 年，學測 88, 94 年，指考 95, 99 年)

> as + sure
> *to* + 確定

attach 〔 ə'tætʃ 〕 *v.* 貼上

She *attached* a note to the door by using the tape. (聯考 53, 67, 82 年，學測 85, 93, 101 年，指考 91 年)

attain 〔 ə'ten 〕 *v.* 達到

One key factor in success is to have a definite goal first and then do your best to *attain* the goal. (聯考 67, 85, 87, 89 年，學測 87 年，指考 95 年)

attract〔ə'trækt〕 v. 吸引

His unusual behavior was intended to *attract* the attention of that girl, but she paid no attention to him.

(模考 82 年，聯考 48, 50, 66, 77, 79, 84, 90 年，學測 84, 86, 88, 90, 91 ①②, 92 ①, 93, 94, 96, 97, 100, 101, 102 年，指考 92, 94, 97, 98, 99, 100, 101, 102 年)

```
at  + tract
 |      |
 to  +  拉
```

attribute〔ə'trɪbjʊt〕 v. 歸因於

He *attributed* his success to his mother.

(模考 91 年，聯考 45, 60 年，學測 84, 100 年，指考 98 年)

authorize〔'ɔθəˌraɪz〕 v. 授權

He *authorized* his lawyer to act for him and make all the decisions. (聯考 51, 65, 78 年，學測 85, 94 年，指考 92, 93 ①, 98, 100 年)

awake〔ə'wek〕 v. 吵醒

The baby was *awoken* by the sound of the doorbell. (聯考 45 年，學測 86, 88, 91 ①, 99, 101 年，指考 102 年)

award 〔ə'wɔrd〕 *v.* 頒發

He was *awarded* the first prize in the speech contest. (聯考 80, 90 年,學測 92 ② 年,指考 95, 97, 100 年)

B b

bend 〔bɛnd〕 *v.* 使彎曲

Superman is so strong that he can *bend* an iron bar into an S shape. (聯考 56, 82, 84 年,指考 102 年)

blame 〔blem〕 *v.* 責備

His boss *blamed* him for having neglected his duty. (聯考 89, 90 年,學測 84 年,指考 97 年)

blend 〔blɛnd〕 *v.* 混合

Oil does not *blend* with water. (學測 96 年)

block 〔blɑk〕 *v.* 堵塞

We were informed that the road was *blocked* by the heavy snow. (聯考 52, 64, 88 年,學測 83, 86, 92 ②, 97, 100 年,指考 91, 97, 102 年)

bloom〔blum〕v. 開花

Flowers *bloom* beautifully in the valley.

(聯考 90 年，學測 93 年，指考 94 年)

blush〔blʌʃ〕v. 臉紅

Jenny *blushed* when praised by her teacher for writing an excellent composition.

(聯考 90 年)

boast〔bost〕v. 自誇

She always *boasts* that her father is the president of a company.   (指考 94 年)

broaden〔'brɔdn̩〕v. 擴展

This TV program will *broaden* young viewers' understanding of the changing world.   (學測 86, 101 年)

C c

capture 〔'kæptʃɚ〕 v. 捕捉

My younger brother went out to the yard to *capture* a butterfly. (聯考 67, 87 年，學測 98, 101 年，

指考 100, 102 年)

cease 〔 sis 〕 v. 停止

The French have *ceased* fighting and asked for peace negotiations. (聯考 49, 73 年，學測 100 年)

charge 〔 tʃɑrdʒ 〕 v. 控告

John was very upset because he was *charged* by the police with breaking the law. (聯考 48, 52, 78, 87 年，學測 83, 92 ②, 102 年，指考 91, 92, 101 年)

civilize 〔'sɪvḷ‚aɪz 〕 v. 教化

One of the main goals of the colonies was to *civilize* the natives.

(聯考 57, 58, 68 年)

civil	+ ize
有禮的	+ v.

- [ ] broaden _____
- [ ] assure _____
- [ ] charge _____
- [ ] argue _____
- [ ] attain _____

- [ ] arise _____
- [ ] assign _____
- [ ] attach _____
- [ ] bend _____
- [ ] blush _____

- [ ] blame _____
- [ ] assume _____
- [ ] awake _____
- [ ] bloom _____
- [ ] block _____

Check List

1. 頒　發　　a ___award___ d
2. 控　告　　c _____ e
3. 授　權　　a _____ e
4. 聯　想　　a _____ e
5. 捕　捉　　c _____ e

6. 教　化　　c _____ e
7. 贊　成　　a _____ e
8. 歸因於　　a _____ e
9. 自　誇　　b _____ t
10. 保　證　　a _____ e

11. 裝　配　　a _____ e
12. 停　止　　c _____ e
13. 混　合　　b _____ d
14. 吸　引　　a _____ t
15. 擴　展　　b _____ n

clarify 〔'klærə,faɪ〕 v. 澄清

The chairman asked the speaker to *clarify* just what he meant. (學測 91①年，指考 100 年)

```
clar + ify
  |     |
clear +  v.
```

classify 〔'klæsə,faɪ〕 v. 分類

The books are *classified* by subjects in the library. (聯考 66 年，指考 93①, 94 年)

collapse 〔kə'læps〕 v. 倒塌

The bridge *collapsed* under the weight of the heavy truck. (學測 85, 89, 94, 99, 100, 102 年，指考 93②, 101 年)

collide 〔kə'laɪd〕 v. 相撞

A taxi *collided* with the bus and five people were injured. (模考 91 年，學測 84, 92①, 102 年，指考 100 年)

combine 〔kəm'baɪn〕 v. 結合

To finish the work, they had to *combine* their efforts. (學測 85, 92①, 96 年，指考 92, 93①, 96, 97, 98, 101, 102 年)

commit 〔kə'mɪt〕 v. 犯（罪）

Has he *committed* any crime before? (聯考 50, 53, 67, 78, 82 年，學測 92 ① 年，指考 95, 96, 99, 100, 101 年)

communicate 〔kə'mjunə,ket〕 v. 溝通

Many parents find it difficult to *communicate* with their children. (聯考 70, 76, 82, 83, 88, 89, 90 年，學測 83, 85, 90, 91 ②, 93, 94, 96, 99, 100, 101 年，指考 93 ①, 95, 96, 98, 99, 100, 101 年)

compare 〔kəm'pɛr〕 v. 比較

He *compared* the two cameras carefully before buying. (模考 82, 91 年，聯考 60, 64, 71, 76, 90 年，學測 90, 92 ①, 94, 101 年，指考 91, 93 ②, 94, 95, 97, 99 年)

compensate 〔'kɑmpən,set〕 v. 彌補

I tried to *compensate* for my forgetfulness by getting Peter some books. (聯考 49, 67, 86 年，學測 88, 96 年，指考 93 ②, 98 年)

compliment 〔'kɑmplə,mɛnt 〕 v. 稱讚

All her teachers *complimented* Mary as she graduated with honors. (聯考 81 年，學測 87, 93 年)

compose 〔 kəm'poz 〕 v. 組成

The committee is *composed* of 50 members.

(模考 82 年，聯考 45, 62, 90 年，
學測 92 ①②, 97, 98, 101, 102 年，
指考 98, 100, 101, 102 年)

```
com + pose
 |      |
all  + put
```

conceal 〔 kən'sil 〕 v. 隱藏

She *concealed* her fear and tried to speak in a calm voice. (模考 82 年，指考 98 年)

concentrate 〔'kɑnsn̩,tret 〕 v. 專心

You must *concentrate* your attention on what you are reading. (聯考 64, 67, 69, 73, 76, 90 年，

學測 85, 88, 89, 101 年，指考 91 年)

concern 〔 kənˈsɝn 〕 *v.* 關心

You have a mother who really *concerns* about you. (模考 82 年，聯考 53, 63, 67, 69, 73, 75, 77, 84, 87, 88, 90 年，學測 86, 87, 91 ②, 95, 96, 98, 99, 102 年，指考 92, 93 ①, 94, 98, 101, 102 年)

condense 〔 kənˈdɛns 〕 *v.* 濃縮

The report is much too long — you must *condense* it, using as few words as possible.

con + dense
   | |
all + 濃密的

(聯考 78, 83 年，指考 95 年)

conduct 〔 kənˈdʌkt 〕 *v.* 經營

His father *conducts* a successful business in the United States. (聯考 48, 59, 80, 88 年，學測 88, 91 ①, 100, 102 年，指考 92, 93 ②, 99, 100, 101, 102 年)

confess 〔 kənˈfɛs 〕 *v.* 承認

She *confessed* she had made a big mistake.

(學測 101 年，指考 91, 97 年)

confine 〔kənˈfaɪn〕 v. 限制

People living in Taipei are being *confined* more and more to office buildings and homes. (聯考 45, 47, 88 年，學測 101 年)

confirm 〔kənˈfɜm〕 v. 確認

I would like to *confirm* the reservation made on Tuesday. (模考 91 年，聯考 80 年，學測 85, 93, 94, 96 年，指考 96 年)

confront 〔kənˈfrʌnt〕 v. 面對

He confessed when *confronted* with the evidence of his guilt.

(聯考 87 年)

con	+ front
together +	前面

connect 〔kəˈnɛkt〕 v. 連接

A highway *connects* the two remote towns.

(聯考 50, 67, 71, 72, 80, 87 年，學測 84, 86, 87, 89, 91 ②, 92 ②, 94, 96, 97, 100, 101, 102 年，指考 91, 95, 96, 97, 100 年)

conquer〔'kɑŋkɚ〕v. 征服

That country was *conquered* by the invaders.

(聯考 47, 53 年,指考 93 ① 年)

conserve〔kən'sɝv〕v. 保存

We have to *conserve* water because of the
water shortage.   (模考 83 年,聯考 85 年,學測 91 ①, 92 ② 年,

指考 91, 99 年)

```
con + serve        con + sist
 |      |           |      |
all  + keep        all  + stand
```

consist〔kən'sɪst〕v. 組成

The committee *consists* of scientists and
engineers.   (聯考 62, 87 年,學測 87, 92 ①, 94, 98, 99 年,

指考 94, 100 年)

console〔kən'sol〕v. 安慰

The policeman *consoled* the lost child by
speaking kindly to her.   (聯考 45 年)

- [ ] commit _____
- [ ] console _____
- [ ] confess _____
- [ ] confirm _____
- [ ] conceal _____

- [ ] condense _____
- [ ] collide _____
- [ ] compose _____
- [ ] confine _____
- [ ] conquer _____

- [ ] clarify _____
- [ ] compare _____
- [ ] combine _____
- [ ] compensate _____
- [ ] conduct _____

Check List

1. 連　接　c ___*connect*___ t
2. 保　存　c _____ e
3. 濃　縮　c _____ e
4. 專　心　c _____ e
5. 溝　通　c _____ e

6. 組　成　c _____ t
7. 分　類　c _____ y
8. 彌　補　c _____ e
9. 關　心　c _____ n
10. 面　對　c _____ t

11. 稱　讚　c _____ t
12. 倒　塌　c _____ e
13. 安　慰　c _____ e
14. 比　較　c _____ e
15. 澄　清　c _____ y

conspire 〔 kən'spaɪr 〕 v. 陰謀

The gangsters *conspired* to rob a bank but were arrested before they did so.

construct 〔 kən'strʌkt 〕 v. 建造

A team of workers are *constructing* the bridge day and night.

(模考 83 年，聯考 66, 73, 80, 84, 87 年，學測 86, 94, 96, 97 年，指考 91, 92, 93 ②, 94, 101, 102 年)

```
con + struct
 |       |
all  + build
```

consult 〔 kən'sʌlt 〕 v. 請教

If your baby is losing weight, you should *consult* your doctor promptly. (聯考 51, 84, 90 年，學測 91 ① 年，指考 94, 96, 101 年)

consume 〔 kən'sjum 〕 v. 消耗

I don't want the car, because this kind of car *consumes* a lot of gas. (模考 91 年，聯考 73 年，學測 89, 90, 92 ②, 96, 97, 99, 100, 102 年，指考 97 年，)

contain 〔 kən'ten 〕 *v.* 包含

The shows on TV often *contain* many violent scenes. (聯考 49, 60, 67, 76, 79, 80, 81, 83, 85, 87 年，學測 87, 89, 92 ②, 96, 97, 98, 99, 100, 101 年，指考 91, 92, 93 ②, 95 年)

contrast 〔 kən'træst 〕 *v.* 對比

The tropical climate *contrasts* sharply with the climate at the North Pole. (聯考 62, 70, 88 年，學測 85, 87, 91 ②, 99 年，指考 91, 95, 99 年)

contribute 〔 kən'trɪbjut 〕 *v.* 貢獻

He *contributes* a lot of money and effort to the neighborhood. (聯考 64, 68, 69, 70, 71, 74, 80, 83, 87 年，學測 88, 90, 91 ①, 92 ②, 93, 99, 102 年，指考 93 ①, 96, 98, 100, 101, 102 年)

convey 〔 kən've 〕 *v.* 傳達

During the conference the speaker tried to *convey* his feelings concerning the urgency of a favorable decision. (聯考 80, 88 年，學測 92 ② 年，指考 95, 99, 101, 102 年)

convict〔kən'vɪkt〕v. 定罪

The prisoner was *convicted* of murder.

(聯考 47, 67 年)

convince〔kən'vɪns〕v. 使相信

We tried to *convince* him of the dangers of smoking, but in vain. (聯考 67, 68, 69 年，學測 88, 92 ①, 94, 96, 97 年，指考 98, 101 年)

cope〔kop〕v. 應付

Nations all over the world today are trying their best to *cope* with the energy crisis.

(聯考 54, 71, 90 年，學測 97, 100 年，指考 96, 98, 101 年)

correspond〔͵kɔrə'spɑnd〕v. 通信

Today members of various pen pal clubs *correspond* with people throughout the world. (聯考 81 年，學測 98 年，指考 97 年)

```
 cor   + respond
  |        |
together + 回應 ( 彼此有回應 )
```

count〔kaʊnt〕v. 重要

One individual does not *count* much in this situation. We have to rely on the collective.

(聯考 54, 56, 61, 74, 77, 81, 90 年，學測 89, 96, 99 年，指考 100, 102 年)

cram〔kræm〕v. 填塞

I *crammed* my bag with a lot of stuff. (聯考 63 年)

crash〔kræʃ〕v. 撞毀

A plane *crashed* in a residential area and caused a lot of damage. (聯考 46, 56 年，學測 91 ①②, 102 年，指考 91, 92 年)

crawl〔krɔl〕v. 爬行

A baby *crawls* before he learns to walk.

(聯考 62 年，學測 85, 89 年，指考 91 年)

cripple〔ˈkrɪpl̩〕v. 使殘廢

He was *crippled* because of a car accident.

(聯考 84 年)

criticize〔ˈkrɪtəˌsaɪz〕 v. 批評

The program was bitterly *criticized* by the
public. (聯考 49, 52, 54, 63, 66, 87 年,學測 83, 86, 88, 89, 91 ①, 96, 98 年,
指考 92, 93 ①, 94, 98, 99, 101 年)

crouch〔krautʃ〕 v. 蹲伏

If there is smoke, *crouch*, do not crawl, as
you go. (聯考 90 年)

crush〔krʌʃ〕 v. 壓碎

The box was *crushed* when the car ran over it.

(學測 84 年,指考 101 年)

cultivate〔ˈkʌltəˌvet〕 v. 培養

If the methods are correct, the ability to
read English is not difficult to *cultivate*.

(模考 83 年,聯考 50, 51, 53, 69, 70, 85, 87 年,學測 91 ①②, 93, 95, 101 年,
指考 92, 93 ②, 94, 101 年)

D d

daydream ('de͵drim) *v.* 做白日夢

May prefers to *daydream* rather than make an effort.

deal (dil) *v.* 交易

The company *deals* mainly in used cars.

(聯考 61, 63, 72, 83, 87 年，學測 86, 97, 98, 99, 101 年，指考 91, 98, 100 年)

decay (dɪ'ke) *v.* 腐敗

Food *decays* in hot weather. (聯考 72, 87 年)

deceive (dɪ'siv) *v.* 欺騙

Frank was *deceiving* me when he told me that I had been fired by our boss. (聯考 81 年，學測 90, 93 年)

declare (dɪ'klɛr) *v.* 宣布

When will they *declare* the result?
Everybody is eager to know who the winner is. (聯考 58 年，學測 88, 89, 93 年)

自 我 測 驗

- [ ] decay   _____
- [ ] conspire   _____
- [ ] crush   _____
- [ ] deal   _____
- [ ] cope   _____

- [ ] convey   _____
- [ ] consult   _____
- [ ] count   _____
- [ ] cram   _____
- [ ] daydream   _____

- [ ] crawl   _____
- [ ] correspond   _____
- [ ] contain   _____
- [ ] convict   _____
- [ ] crouch   _____

Check List

1. 消　耗　　c ___*consume*___ e
2. 貢　獻　　c _____ e
3. 壓　碎　　c _____ h
4. 欺　騙　　d _____ e
5. 培　養　　c _____ e

6. 批　評　　c _____ e
7. 通　信　　c _____ d
8. 陰　謀　　c _____ e
9. 對　比　　c _____ t
10. 使相信　　c _____ e

11. 使殘廢　　c _____ e
12. 宣　布　　d _____ e
13. 建　造　　c _____ t
14. 腐　敗　　d _____ y
15. 撞　毀　　c _____ h

decline 〔 dɪ'klaɪn 〕 v. 婉拒

I had to *decline* his kind
invitation to the dinner on
account of urgent business.

```
de   + cline
 |       |
down + 傾斜
```

(模考 83 年，聯考 64, 69, 73, 75, 85, 86 年，學測 99 年，指考 93 ②, 99, 100 年)

dedicate 〔'dɛdə,ket 〕 v. 奉獻

Miss Chang *dedicated* most of her time to
taking care of stray animals. (學測 99 年)

defeat 〔 dɪ'fit 〕 v. 擊敗

Our team *defeated* our opponents by a
score of 3 to 0. (模考 82, 83 年，聯考 47, 51, 65, 88 年，

學測 91 ①, 92 ①, 96 年，指考 94, 98, 101 年)

defend 〔 dɪ'fɛnd 〕 v. 保護

They couldn't fight back, but could only
defend themselves. (模考 82 年，聯考 47, 65, 67, 73, 85, 89 年，

學測 96, 97 年，指考 91, 102 年)

delay〔dɪ'le〕v. 延誤

I was *delayed* by a traffic jam on the freeway for about an hour. (聯考 48, 65, 80, 88 年，學測 85, 92 ①, 97 年，指考 92 年)

delight〔dɪ'laɪt〕v. 使高興

The performance of the musicians has really *delighted* all of us. (模考 91 年，聯考 74, 78, 79, 86, 87, 88 年，學測 87, 89, 90, 96, 100 年，指考 93 ①, 94, 102 年)

deny〔dɪ'naɪ〕v. 否認

He *denied* that he had stolen the bicycle. (聯考 53, 67 年，指考 100 年)

depart〔dɪ'pɑrt〕v. 離開

The plane is scheduled to *depart* at nine sharp. (聯考 66, 71, 86, 88 年，學測 86, 92 ②, 99 年，指考 101 年)

depend〔dɪ'pɛnd〕v. 視…而定

Success *depends* on your efforts and ability. (聯考 46, 51, 53, 69, 71, 76 年，學測 88, 92 ②, 94, 96, 101, 102 年，指考 98, 99 年)

deprive 〔 dɪ'praɪv 〕 v. 剝奪

He was *deprived* of his sight by the accident.

(模考 91 年，聯考 69 年，指考 95 年)

describe 〔 dɪ'skraɪb 〕 v. 描述

These events are accurately *described* in the

newspaper. (聯考 47, 48, 59, 62, 73, 76,

78, 81, 84, 85, 88 年，學測 85, 87, 88, 91 ①, 92 ①,

93, 98, 99, 101 年，指考 91, 94, 96, 97, 98, 99 年)

de	+ scribe
|	|
down	+ *write*

desert 〔 dɪ'zɝt 〕 v. 拋棄

You should not *desert* your friends when

they're in trouble. (聯考 45, 46, 54, 56, 58, 59, 61, 66, 68, 80, 86,

88 年，學測 93, 94 年，指考 91, 95, 102 年)

deserve 〔 dɪ'zɝv 〕 v. 應得

He has been working very hard, and so he

deserves a vacation. (模考 83 年，聯考 49, 61, 64, 73, 86 年，

學測 83, 86, 88, 93, 96 年，指考 93 ②, 101 年)

despise ﹝ dɪ'spaɪz ﹞ *v.* 輕視

Should you *despise* him just because his family is poor? (聯考 49 年)

destroy ﹝ dɪ'strɔɪ ﹞ *v.* 破壞

The fire that lasted five days *destroyed* the whole forest. (聯考 48, 53, 63, 67, 69, 71, 81, 83, 87, 88 年，學測 83, 86, 89, 90, 96, 97 年，指考 96, 97, 98, 99, 101, 102 年)

detect ﹝ dɪ'tɛkt ﹞ *v.* 偵測

The device is designed to *detect* smoke and then sound the alarm. (聯考 49, 65, 84 年，學測 85, 90, 96, 100, 102 年，指考 91, 92, 93 ①, 100, 101 年)

deter ﹝ dɪ'tɝ ﹞ *v.* 阻礙

Bad weather *deterred* us from going on a hike. (指考 92 年)

devote ﹝ dɪ'vot ﹞ *v.* 致力於

Diane *devoted* her life to the study of gorillas.

(模考 91 年，聯考 64, 67 年，學測 83, 96 年，指考 91, 94, 96, 97, 99 年)

diagnose 〔͵daɪəgˈnoz 〕 *v.* 診斷

A doctor has to *diagnose* your illness
before giving you a prescription. (聯考 86, 87,
89 年，學測 87 年，指考 96, 97 年)

diminish 〔 dəˈmɪnɪʃ 〕 *v.* 減少

His income *diminished* because he got ill and
took a month's sick leave. (模考 91 年，學測 83, 96 年)

disagree 〔͵dɪsəˈgri 〕 *v.* 意見不合

We cannot decide; we *disagree* about
everything. (模考 83 年，聯考 50, 51, 62, 73, 78, 81 年，學測 94 年)

disappoint 〔͵dɪsəˈpɔɪnt 〕 *v.* 使失望

In order not to *disappoint* her parents,
she is doing her best to get into her
ideal college. (聯考 50, 51, 60, 61, 66, 75, 81, 86, 87 年，學測 91 ①,
94, 96, 100 年，指考 92, 95, 100 年)

```
dis + appoint
 |      |
not +  指派 ( 沒有被派到工作 )
```

discourage 〔dɪsˈkɝɪdʒ〕 *v.* 使氣餒

He is a person who is not easily *discouraged* by failures. (聯考 64, 76 年，學測 84, 96 年，指考 92 年)

disguise 〔dɪsˈgaɪz〕 *v.* 偽裝

She *disguised* herself as a man with a false beard. (聯考 63 年，學測 94 年，指考 92, 95, 101 年)

dismiss 〔dɪsˈmɪs〕 *v.* 解散

The teacher *dismissed* the class when the bell rang. (聯考 66, 79, 82 年，學測 83, 88, 102 年，指考 91, 93 ②, 97 年)

dispose 〔dɪˈspoz〕 *v.* 處理

How and where to *dispose* of garbage is a major issue for the city government. (模考 82 年，聯考 84, 88 年，學測 86, 92 ①②年)

dissolve 〔dɪˈzɑlv〕 *v.* 溶解

Sugar and salt *dissolve* in water. (模考 91 年，指考 96 年)

- [ ] delay _____
- [ ] deny _____
- [ ] devote _____
- [ ] dismiss _____
- [ ] dedicate _____

- [ ] defeat _____
- [ ] desert _____
- [ ] detect _____
- [ ] dispose _____
- [ ] deter _____

- [ ] despise _____
- [ ] depend _____
- [ ] delight _____
- [ ] depart _____
- [ ] disagree _____

Check List

1. 保　護　　d ___defend___ d
2. 使氣餒　　d _____ e
3. 婉　拒　　d _____ e
4. 擊　敗　　d _____ t
5. 描　述　　d _____ e

6. 破　壞　　d _____ y
7. 診　斷　　d _____ e
8. 使失望　　d _____ t
9. 應　得　　d _____ e
10. 剝　奪　　d _____ e

11. 減　少　　d _____ h
12. 偽　裝　　d _____ e
13. 溶　解　　d _____ e
14. 離　開　　d _____ t
15. 致力於　　d _____ e

distinguish 〔 dɪ'stɪŋgwɪʃ 〕 *v.* 區分

Even their mother finds it hard to
distinguish between the twins. (聯考 50, 63, 66, 71 年，

指考 92 ②, 94, 95, 101 年)

distract 〔 dɪ'strækt 〕 *v.* 使分心

The smell of chocolate both
distracts and relaxes people
at the same time. (聯考 90 年)

dis	+ tract
|	|
away	+ 拉

distribute 〔 dɪ'strɪbjut 〕 *v.* 分發

The teacher *distributed* the examination
papers to the class. (模考 82, 83, 91 年，聯考 60, 63, 75, 85,

90, 102 年，學測 92 ②, 93, 96, 102 年)

disturb 〔 dɪ'stɝb 〕 *v.* 打擾

Mr. Smith won't tolerate
talking in class; he says it
disturbs others. (聯考 61, 64, 69,

（ p.161～p.250 ）

78, 87, 90 年，學測 83, 87, 90, 94 年，指考 94, 96 年)

divide 〔 dəˈvaɪd 〕 *v.* 分開

The robbers *divided* the money equally among themselves. (聯考 46, 48, 51, 53, 58, 62, 78, 83, 90 年，學測 88, 96, 99, 100, 101 年，指考 94, 93 ①②, 102 年)

dominate 〔ˈdɑməˌnet 〕 *v.* 支配

Mr. Jackson is the sole leader of the group. He *dominates* the other members. (聯考 86, 87 年，學測 91 ① 年)

download 〔ˈdaʊnˌlod 〕 *v.* 下載

I can use my computer to *download* some software from the Internet. (指考 91, 98, 102 年)

E e

eliminate 〔 ɪˈlɪməˌnet 〕 *v.* 消除

We worked carefully to *eliminate* any possibility of mistakes. (聯考 83, 89 年，學測 92 ②, 93 年，指考 93 ①, 98, 101 年)

embarrass 〔 ɪm'bærəs 〕 *v.* 使困窘

They *embarrassed* the speaker with their misleading questions. (聯考 72, 87 年,學測 88, 89 年,指考 101 年)

embrace 〔 ɪm'bres 〕 *v.* 擁抱

When he returned safely, his mother *embraced* him tightly. (聯考 81 年,學測 96, 98 年,指考 92 年)

emigrate 〔'ɛmə‚gret 〕 *v.* 移出

Many people *emigrated* from Germany to the United States after the rise of Hitler.

e	+ migr	+ ate
out	*move*	*v.*

enchant 〔 ɪn'tʃænt 〕 *v.* 使著迷

She was *enchanted* by the lovely dancing children.

encounter 〔ɪn'kaʊntɚ〕 v. 遭遇

I am ready to *encounter* dangers in the course of this expedition. (聯考 71, 88 年, 學測 87 年, 指考 93① 年)

encourage 〔ɪn'kɝɪdʒ〕 v. 鼓勵

When I don't do well on exams, my mother always *encourages* me to study harder.

(模考 82, 83 年, 聯考 49, 73, 76, 80, 82, 83, 87, 88 年, 學測 83, 84, 85, 86, 87, 91②, 94, 96 年, 指考 91, 92, 93②, 95, 96, 98, 100, 102 年)

endure 〔ɪn'djʊr〕 v. 持續

He is a great writer, and his books will *endure* forever. (聯考 68, 73 年, 學測 86, 100 年, 指考 98, 102 年)

enforce 〔ɪn'fors〕 v. 實施

Traffic regulations should be strictly *enforced*. (指考 93②, 100 年)

en + fore
  | |
in + 力量

engage 〔ɪn'gedʒ〕 v. 從事

He *engaged* in the study of ecology. (聯考 47, 51, 56, 81, 87 年, 學測 86 年)

enlarge 〔 ɪn'lɑrdʒ 〕 v. 放大

These two photographs are too small. Let's have them *enlarged*. (聯考 67,84 年，學測 91 ② 年)

enrich 〔 ɪn'rɪtʃ 〕 v. 充實

If you can afford to travel to Europe, it will *enrich* your education. (聯考 49 年)

equip 〔 ɪ'kwɪp 〕 v. 裝備

The company *equipped* their stereos with a new device. (聯考 47,78 年，學測 83,86,88,90,94,101,102 年，指考 91,93 ①②,95,99 年)

erect 〔 ɪ'rɛkt 〕 v. 建造

They plan to *erect* a monument in honor of the hero. (學測 87 年)

erupt 〔 ɪ'rʌpt 〕 v. 爆發

The volcano *erupted*, sending a slow-moving flow of lava through the town. (模考 91 年，聯考 71 年)

```
e   + rupt
|     |
out + break
```

escape 〔ə'skep〕*v.* 逃走

Several criminals planned to *escape* from prison, but failed. (聯考 46, 50, 59, 62, 66, 68 年，學測 83, 91 ①②, 93, 97, 100, 102 年，指考 93 ①, 102 年)

escort 〔ɪ'skɔrt〕*v.* 護送

When Mrs. Jones left the party, her host *escorted* her to the gate. (學測 88 年，指考 101, 102 年)

establish 〔ə'stæblɪʃ〕*v.* 建立

We hope to *establish* friendly relations with as many countries as possible. (聯考 46, 49, 61, 67, 73 年，學測 83, 86, 96, 101 年，指考 91, 93 ①, 94, 96, 97 年)

estimate 〔'ɛstə,met〕*v.* 估計

I *estimated* that it would take four hours to get there by bus. (聯考 64, 70, 77 年，學測 88, 91 ①, 92 ①②, 98, 99, 102 年，指考 91, 93 ②, 98, 99 年)

- [ ] erect _____
- [ ] dominate _____
- [ ] equip _____
- [ ] disturb _____
- [ ] erupt _____

- [ ] escort _____
- [ ] divide _____
- [ ] enchant _____
- [ ] engage _____
- [ ] escape _____

- [ ] eliminate _____
- [ ] embrace _____
- [ ] enforce _____
- [ ] enrich _____
- [ ] distribute _____

Check List

1. 逃　走　　e ___escape___ e
2. 使分心　　d _____ t
3. 使困窘　　e _____ s
4. 遭　遇　　e _____ r
5. 放　大　　e _____ e

6. 建　立　　e _____ h
7. 區　分　　d _____ h
8. 估　計　　e _____ e
9. 鼓　勵　　e _____ e
10. 下　載　　d _____ d

11. 移　出　　e _____ e
12. 支　配　　d _____ e
13. 消　除　　e _____ e
14. 分　發　　d _____ e
15. 持　續　　e _____ e

exaggerate 〔 ɪgˈzædʒəˌret 〕 v. 誇大

If you always *exaggerate*, people will no longer believe you. (模考 82, 91 年，聯考 66, 68 年，

學測 91 ② 年)

examine 〔 ɪgˈzæmɪn 〕 v. 檢查

You have to *examine* these bills and check each item before you pay. (聯考 46, 49, 50, 62, 75, 84, 90 年，

學測 86, 87 年，指考 91, 99, 100, 101 年)

exceed 〔 ɪkˈsid 〕 v. 超過

You will have trouble if the amount of money you spend *exceeds* the amount you earn. (聯考 49, 71 年，學測 92 ① 年，指考 96, 97 年)

```
ex  + ceed
 |      |
out  +  go
```

excel 〔 ɪkˈsɛl 〕 v. 擅長

He *excels* in English. (聯考 70 年，學測 93 年)

exclude 〔 ɪk'sklud 〕 *v.* 排除

He was *excluded* from the school team
for his misbehavior. (聯考 49, 59, 67 年，學測 93 年，

指考 93 ①, 95, 96, 98 年)

ex + clude
 | |
out + *close*

exist 〔 ɪg'zɪst 〕 *v.* 存在

Do you believe life *exists* on Mars? (聯考 45, 48,

67, 68, 69 年，學測 84, 90, 93, 97, 102 年，指考 92, 93 ①②, 94, 95, 100, 102 年)

expand 〔 ɪk'spænd 〕 *v.* 擴大

It was necessary to *expand* the factory
because the company was doing more
business. (模考 83 年，聯考 83, 84, 86 年，學測 88, 93, 94, 96 年，

指考 93 ①, 97, 98, 100, 102 年)

expire 〔 ɪk'spaɪr 〕 *v.* 期滿

My passport *expired* last month and I have
to have it renewed.

explode 〔 ɪk'splod 〕 v. 爆炸

Karen blew up the balloon until it *exploded* in her face. (模考 91 年，聯考 49 年，學測 84, 92 ①, 94 年，指考 92, 101, 102 年)

explore 〔 ɪk'splor 〕 v. 探險

They organized a team to *explore* the newly discovered island. (模考 91 年，聯考 57, 69, 81 年，學測 91 ①, 92 ②, 96, 101 年，指考 92, 93 ①, 98, 99, 100 年)

expose 〔 ɪk'spoz 〕 v. 暴露

People *exposed* to noise for a long time run the risk of impaired hearing. (模考 91 年，

```
ex + pose
 |      |
out + put
```

聯考 50, 57, 62, 68 年，學測 92 ②, 98, 99 年，指考 98, 101 年)

extend 〔 ɪk'stɛnd 〕 v. 延伸

Because the discussion took a long time, they *extended* the meeting for another 20 minutes. (聯考 48, 75 年，學測 98 年，指考 94, 98 年)

F f

facilitate 〔 fəˈsɪləˌtet 〕 v. 使便利

The reason for designing the special bus lane is to *facilitate* the traffic flow, not to slow it down. (聯考 68, 89 年，學測 84, 99 年，指考 102 年)

faint 〔 fent 〕 v. 暈倒

She almost *fainted* when she saw her idol up close during his latest concert in Taipei.

(學測 86 年)

fascinate 〔ˈfæsṇˌet 〕 v. 使著迷

East Asians have been *fascinated* with kites for many centuries. (聯考 48, 65, 66, 79, 89 年，學測 90, 91 ①, 92 ① 年，指考 95, 97, 101, 102 年)

figure 〔ˈfɪgjɚ 〕 v. 認為

John *figured* himself to be the best candidate for the post. (聯考 50, 65, 70, 73, 75, 81 年，學測 84, 88, 101 年，指考 91, 93 ①②, 94, 95, 96, 97, 100, 101, 102 年)

flourish (ˈflɝɪʃ) *v.* 興盛

The fine arts *flourished* in
Italy in the 15th century.

| flour | + | ish |
| flower | + | *v.* |

(聯考 47, 63, 68, 89 年，學測 92 ① 年，指考 94 年)

forbid (fɚˈbɪd) *v.* 禁止

Because of the recent accidents, our parents
forbid my brother and me to swim in the
river. (聯考 46, 50, 63, 65, 80 年，指考 102 年)

found (faʊnd) *v.* 建立

The university, one of the oldest schools in
the world, was *founded* in 1412. (聯考 51, 52, 69, 72,
73, 87 年，學測 90, 92 ①, 96, 99, 101 年，指考 93 ① ②, 98, 101, 102 年)

fulfill (fʊlˈfɪl) *v.* 履行

He is not a man worthy of trust. He never
fulfills promises he has made to others.

(聯考 68, 88, 89 年，學測 91 ①, 94 年，指考 93 ① 年)

G g

gather 〔'gæðɚ〕 v. 收集

He is *gathering* materials for a new book.

(聯考 59, 75, 87 年，學測 91 ①, 93 年，指考 95, 97, 101 年)

glance 〔 glæns 〕 v. 瞥一眼

Before stealing money from the purse, the little boy *glanced* around in case his mother should catch him. (聯考 64, 83, 88 年，學測 89, 90 年，

指考 94, 95 年)

graduate 〔'grædʒʊ,et 〕 v. 畢業

She *graduated* from college last summer.

(聯考 56, 63, 73, 75, 80, 86 年，學測 84, 87, 90, 96, 99, 100 年，指考 92, 93 ②，

94, 100 年)

grumble 〔'grʌmbḷ 〕 v. 抱怨

He has everything he needs; he has nothing to *grumble* about.

☐ expire   _____

☐ exaggerate   _____

☐ forbid   _____

☐ grumble   _____

☐ expose   _____

☐ found   _____

☐ exclude   _____

☐ glance   _____

☐ flourish   _____

☐ fascinate   _____

☐ exceed   _____

☐ explode   _____

☐ faint   _____

☐ expand   _____

☐ excel   _____

Check List

1.	探　險	e ___explore___	e
2.	延　伸	e _____	d
3.	收　集	g _____	r
4.	畢　業	g _____	e
5.	檢　查	e _____	e
6.	擅　長	e _____	l
7.	瞥一眼	g _____	e
8.	使便利	f _____	e
9.	興　盛	f _____	h
10.	履　行	f _____	l
11.	超　過	e _____	d
12.	擴　大	e _____	d
13.	存　在	e _____	t
14.	爆　炸	e _____	e
15.	認　為	f _____	e

guarantee 〔 ˌgærən'ti 〕 *v.* 保證

The quality of our products is *guaranteed*.

(聯考 48, 65, 69, 73 年，指考 95 年)

H h

hatch 〔 hætʃ 〕 *v.* 孵化

The eggs are *hatched* by the heat of the sun.

hesitate 〔'hɛzəˌtet 〕 *v.* 猶豫

If I can help you with the project, don't
hesitate to call me. (聯考 64, 69, 86, 90 年，學測 87, 91 ①, 96,

97, 99, 101 年，指考 95, 96 年)

horrify 〔'hɔrəˌfaɪ 〕 *v.* 使驚恐

We were *horrified* by such a terrible sight.

(聯考 60, 68, 70 年)

humiliate 〔 hju'mɪlɪˌet 〕 *v.* 羞辱

Jones was accused of murder, which
humiliated all his family members.

I i

identify ﹝aɪˈdɛntəˌfaɪ﹞ *v.* 辨認

It's impossible to *identify* the man among so many people. (模考 91 年，聯考 65, 66, 82 年，學測 93, 98, 99, 100, 102 年，指考 93 ①, 100 年)

ignore ﹝ɪgˈnɔr﹞ *v.* 忽略

I gave him my sincere advice but he *ignored* it. (聯考 54, 62, 66, 68, 69, 73, 79, 86, 87, 89 年，學測 87, 91 ①②, 92 ①, 94, 96, 101 年，指考 92, 93 ②, 95, 99, 100, 101 年)

imitate ﹝ˈɪməˌtet﹞ *v.* 模仿

Don't just *imitate* — try to come up with your own original idea. (模考 83 年，聯考 68, 69, 71, 81, 86, 88 年，學測 92 ②, 98 年)

immigrate ﹝ˈɪməˌgret﹞ *v.* 移入

Many people want to *immigrate* to the United States.

(學測 85, 98, 99 年，指考 97 年)

im	+ migr	+ ate
into	+ *move*	+ *v.*

imply 〔 ɪm'plaɪ 〕 v. 暗示

I can't understand what your words *imply*.

(聯考 66, 71 年，學測 98 年)

impose 〔 ɪm'poz 〕 v. 加於

The government *imposed* new taxes on imported goods. (模考 82 年，聯考 68, 83, 87 年)

impress 〔 ɪm'prɛs 〕 v. 使印象深刻

What *impressed* you most during your visit to the Eiffel Tower? (聯考 62, 66, 69, 73, 79, 84, 86, 88 年，

學測 84, 88, 91 ①, 92 ①, 94, 98, 101 年，指考 94 年)

```
im + press
 |      |
in  +  壓 ( 壓進腦海裏 )
```

indicate 〔 'ɪndə,ket 〕 v. 指出

The research *indicated* that smoking is a possible cause of lung cancer. (聯考 49, 69, 73, 84, 83,

86, 88 年，學測 83, 85, 89, 93, 102 年，指考 92, 98, 100 年)

indulge 〔 ɪnˈdʌldʒ 〕 *v.* 縱容

She *indulged* her son by giving him
everything he wanted. (模考 91 年，聯考 63, 77, 87 年，
指考 93 ①②, 96, 102 年)

inform 〔 ɪnˈfɔrm 〕 *v.* 通知

We were *informed* that two prisoners had
escaped. (模考 91 年，聯考 45, 87 年，學測 88, 93, 94, 98 年，
指考 93 ①, 94, 96, 99, 101 年)

inhabit 〔 ɪnˈhæbɪt 〕 *v.* 居住

Different kinds of fish *inhabit* the deep
waters. (聯考 53, 56, 57, 62, 82 年，指考 94 年)

inherit 〔 ɪnˈhɛrɪt 〕 *v.* 繼承

Michelle *inherited* her father's business.

(聯考 50, 64, 70 年，指考 92 年)

inquire 〔 ɪnˈkwaɪr 〕 *v.* 詢問

She *inquired* of me most courteously
whether I wished to continue. (模考 91 年，聯考 49,
56, 69, 86 年，學測 87 年，指考 92 年)

insert 〔 ɪn'sɝt 〕 v. 插入

Phil always tries to *insert* humor into a
tense situation. (聯考 88, 90 年)

insist 〔 ɪn'sɪst 〕 v. 堅持

My mother *insisted* that I go on with my
education. (聯考 53, 56, 61, 68, 71, 72 年，學測 86, 88, 90, 94, 99 年，

指考 102 年)

inspire 〔 ɪn'spaɪr 〕 v. 鼓舞

The story of Helen Keller *inspired* us to
make greater efforts. (聯考 47, 64, 72, 73, 87 年，學測 86,

90, 97, 101 年，指考 91, 92, 99, 101, 102 年)

```
in  + spire
 |     |
in  + breathe (吹氣進入)
```

install 〔 ɪn'stɔl 〕 v. 安裝

A new machine has been *installed* in the
laboratory. (聯考 62, 90 年，學測 87, 92 ① 年，指考 93 ②, 101 年)

integrate 〔'ɪntə‚gret 〕 *v.* 融合

The child was only adopted a year ago, but he has completely *integrated* into the family.

intend 〔 ɪn'tɛnd 〕 *v.* 打算

He *intends* to go to Paris and learn French.

(聯考 46, 47, 51, 67, 71, 90 年，學測 88, 91 ①, 92 ②, 93, 98, 101 年，指考 96 年)

intensify 〔 ɪn'tɛnsə‚faɪ 〕 *v.* 加強

Her illness *intensified* and she was transferred to the intensive care unit. (學測 88, 90, 91 ①②, 92 ②, 97, 99, 100 年，指考 93 ①, 94, 96, 97, 99 年)

```
in  +  tens  + ify
|        |      |
in  + stretch +  v.
```

interpret 〔 ɪn'tɝprɪt 〕 *v.* 解釋

This poem may be *interpreted* in several different ways. (模考 83 年，聯考 48, 67, 79 年，學測 90, 99, 100, 101 年，指考 95, 97, 99, 101 年)

自我測驗

- [ ] inform   _____
- [ ] inquire   _____
- [ ] install   _____
- [ ] hatch   _____
- [ ] impress   _____

- [ ] impose   _____
- [ ] identify   _____
- [ ] horrify   _____
- [ ] intend   _____
- [ ] insert   _____

- [ ] insist   _____
- [ ] indicate   _____
- [ ] imitate   _____
- [ ] humiliate   _____
- [ ] inhabit   _____

Check List

1. 忽　略　i ___*ignore*___ e
2. 猶　豫　h _____ e
3. 縱　容　i _____ e
4. 繼　承　i _____ t
5. 鼓　舞　i _____ e
6. 融　合　i _____ e
7. 保　證　g _____ e
8. 模　仿　i _____ e
9. 暗　示　i _____ y
10. 移　入　i _____ e
11. 居　住　i _____ t
12. 加　強　i _____ y
13. 解　釋　i _____ t
14. 羞　辱　h _____ e
15. 安　裝　i _____ l

interview〔ˋɪntɚˏvju〕v. 訪問

Movie stars are usually *interviewed* by reporters about their marriage. (聯考 75 年，學測 88, 91 ①, 100, 101 年，指考 91, 102 年)

inter	+ view
between	+ *see* (面對面)

invade〔ɪnˋved〕v. 侵略

Germany *invaded* many European countries during World War II. (聯考 87 年，學測 94, 97, 100 年，指考 92, 97, 102 年)

invest〔ɪnˋvɛst〕v. 投資

Our country has become hi-tech by *investing* heavily in the electronics industry. (聯考 63, 69, 70, 71, 83, 87, 90 年，學測 91 ②, 98, 102 年，指考 96, 102 年)

involve〔ɪnˋvɑlv〕v. 牽涉

The man was found to have been *involved* in a bank robbery. (模考 91 年，聯考 67, 80, 82, 85, 87, 88 年，學測 85, 91 ②, 92 ②, 97, 98 年，指考 91, 92, 94, 95, 97 年)

irritate 〔'ɪrəˌtet 〕 v. 激怒

His meaningless and stupid questions *irritated* me. (聯考 87 年，學測 98 年，指考 92, 99 年)

isolate 〔'aɪsḷˌet 〕 v. 隔離

The people with contagious diseases were *isolated* immediately. (學測 99 年，指考 92, 96 年)

issue 〔'ɪʃʊ 〕 v. 發行

The magazine is *issued* on the first day of every month. (模考 91 年，聯考 55, 83, 85 年，學測 83, 84, 85, 92 ②, 96, 98, 99, 102 年，指考 91, 93 ①, 94, 95, 98, 99, 101, 102 年)

L l

launch 〔 lɔntʃ, lɑntʃ 〕 v. 發射

The missile was *launched* from the fighter jet. (聯考 47 年，學測 93, 97, 102 年，指考 93 ②, 94, 99 年)

locate 〔 lo'ket 〕 v. 位於

The hotel is *located* on the main shopping street. (學測 90, 96, 97, 98, 99 年，指考 92, 93 ①②, 94, 97, 101, 102 年)

M m

maintain 〔 men'ten 〕 *v.* 維持

Swimming is one of the best ways for a person to *maintain* good health. (聯考 48, 51, 54, 63, 67, 68, 72, 75, 80, 90 年，學測 84, 85, 88, 90, 92 ① ②, 93 ②, 94, 96, 97, 99, 100 年，指考 93 ②, 94, 97, 101 年)

major 〔 'medʒɚ 〕 *v.* 主修

Mike decided to *major* in English in college.

(模考 91 年，聯考 64, 66, 67, 71, 80 年，學測 86, 88, 92 ① ②, 93, 96, 98, 102 年，指考 92, 93 ① ②, 94, 99, 100, 101 年)

manage 〔 'mænɪdʒ 〕 *v.* 設法

Though we ran into a lot of difficulties, we *managed* to get what we wanted. (模考 91 年，聯考 60, 61, 63, 67, 71, 72, 77, 78 年，學測 86, 89, 90, 91 ①, 92 ① ②, 98, 99 年，指考 93 ①, 94, 96, 97, 99, 100, 101, 102 年)

master 〔 'mæstɚ 〕 *v.* 精通

To *master* English, you need a lot of devotion and practice. (聯考 81, 82, 88 年，學測 92 ② 年，指考 91, 99, 101 年)

match 〔 mætʃ 〕 *v.* 相配

This dress *matches* your eyes. (聯考 77, 81, 90 年，

學測 98, 99, 102 年，指考 92, 93 ①②, 101 年)

measure 〔'mɛʒɚ 〕 *v.* 測量

Before you lay a carpet in a room, you have to *measure* the room. (聯考 65, 68, 69, 71, 80, 82, 84, 88 年，

學測 87, 89, 92 ②, 93, 96, 97, 100, 102 年，指考 92, 93 ①②, 95, 98, 100, 101 年)

memorize 〔'mɛmə,raɪz 〕 *v.* 背誦

The hardest work in studying English is to *memorize* a lot of new words and phrases.

(聯考 64, 65, 72, 74, 81, 88 年，學測 85, 88, 92 ②, 97, 101 年，指考 93 ①, 97, 99 年)

migrate 〔'maɪgret 〕 *v.* 遷移

People are wondering how birds find their way when *migrating* south. (模考 83 年，

聯考 84 年，學測 85 年)

migr + ate
| |
move + v.

minimize 〔'mɪnə,maɪz 〕 *v.* 使減到最低

Our government is working on a way to *minimize* the criminal rate. (聯考 65, 68, 69, 88 年，學測 92 ②, 97, 98 年，指考 93 ①, 100, 101 年)

mislead 〔 mɪs'lid 〕 *v.* 誤導

She *misled* the investigators into believing that he died of natural causes. (聯考 70, 84 年，指考 95, 100 年)

N n

neglect 〔 nɪ'glɛkt 〕 *v.* 忽視

What is more serious is that more and more people *neglect* the traffic rules. (聯考 66, 69, 86 年，學測 87, 91 ②, 96 年，指考 98 年)

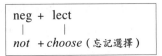

```
neg  +  lect
 |        |
not  + choose（忘記選擇）
```

negotiate 〔 nɪ'goʃɪ,et 〕 *v.* 談判

His personality makes it very difficult to *negotiate* and reach an agreement with him.

(聯考 85, 86 年，學測 90, 96 年，指考 101 年)

O o

object 〔 əb'dʒɛkt 〕 v. 反對

No one present *objected* to his suggestion.

(聯考 45, 50, 52, 61, 63, 65, 66, 69, 71, 72, 78, 87 年，學測 83, 85, 84, 90, 91 ①, 93, 94, 98, 99, 101, 102 年，指考 92 ①, 93 ①, 95, 98, 100, 102 年)

observe 〔 əb'zɝv 〕 v. 觀察

The student carefully *observed* the wane and wax of the moon. (聯考 48, 49, 57, 66, 85 年，學測 88, 92 ①, 93, 99, 101, 102 年，指考 93 ①, 94, 97, 99, 100 年)

obtain 〔 əb'ten 〕 v. 獲得

I am curious about how John *obtained* such a large sum of money. (聯考 66, 75 年，學測 85, 88, 89, 99, 102 年，指考 93, 97 年)

occupy 〔'ɑkjə,paɪ 〕 v. 占據

Much of Europe was *occupied* by Germany during World War II. (學測 97, 101 年，指考 93 ①, 94, 98 年)

自 我 測 驗

- ☐ master _____
- ☐ memorize _____
- ☐ neglect _____
- ☐ object _____
- ☐ occupy _____

- ☐ minimize _____
- ☐ lunch _____
- ☐ involve _____
- ☐ irritate _____
- ☐ migrate _____

- ☐ mislead _____
- ☐ major _____
- ☐ invade _____
- ☐ issue _____
- ☐ observe _____

Check List

1. 相 配　　m ___match___ h
2. 反 對　　o _____ t
3. 佔 據　　o _____ y
4. 測 量　　m _____ e
5. 隔 離　　i _____ e

6. 談 判　　n _____ e
7. 維 持　　m _____ n
8. 投 資　　i _____ t
9. 訪 問　　i _____ w
10. 獲 得　　o _____ n

11. 設 法　　m _____ e
12. 發 行　　i _____ e
13. 侵 略　　i _____ e
14. 背 誦　　m _____ e
15. 位 於　　l _____ e

offend 〔 ə'fɛnd 〕 v. 冒犯

Please forgive me. I didn't mean to
offend you. (聯考 69, 73, 85 年，學測 89 年)

oppose 〔 ə'poz 〕 v. 反對

Is there anyone who *opposes* the plans put
forward by the committee? (聯考 63, 76 年，

學測 91 ①, 102 年，指考 92, 94, 99, 101 年)

organize 〔 'ɔrgən,aɪz 〕 v. 組織

The police *organized* a rescue team to look
for the missing students. (聯考 51, 62, 67, 68, 71, 83, 86, 88,

90 年，學測 92 ①, 96, 98, 99, 101 年，指考 91, 93 ①, 96, 97, 98, 101, 102 年)

originate 〔 ə'rɪdʒə,net 〕 v. 起源

The Industrial Revolution *originated*
from the invention of the
steam engine. (聯考 46, 53, 56, 72, 73, 79,

82, 87, 88 年，學測 84, 85, 90, 91 ①, 92 ②, 93, 94 年，

指考 94, 96, 100 年)

origin	+ ate
|	|
起源	+ v.

overcome 〔͵ovəˊkʌm 〕 v. 克服

If only you work hard, you can *overcome* any difficulty. (模考 82 年，聯考 50, 87 年，學測 90, 91 ①, 101 年，指考 93 ②, 97, 98, 100 年)

P p

panic 〔ˊpænɪk 〕 v. 恐慌

Relax, and above all, don't *panic*. (聯考 50 年，學測 89 年，指考 101 年)

paralyze 〔ˊpærə͵laɪz 〕 v. 使麻痺

Fear *paralyzes* my mind. (聯考 68 年，學測 101 年，指考 91, 94 年)

participate 〔 parˊtɪsə͵pet 〕 v. 參加

Everyone here *participated* in the discussion. (聯考 66, 86, 89 年，學測 83, 89, 91 ②, 98, 99 年，指考 91, 92, 93 ②, 96, 98 年)

perform 〔 pɚ'fɔrm 〕 v. 表演

The magician *performed* his tricks with perfect skill. (聯考 49, 50, 63, 65, 66, 81, 85, 87, 88, 90 年,學測 91 ①, 92 ①, 93, 97, 99, 100, 101 年,指考 95, 97, 100, 101 年)

permit 〔 pɚ'mɪt 〕 v. 允許

Weather *permitting*, we will go on a picnic on Sunday. (聯考 51, 59, 81, 83, 84, 90, 96 年,學測 83, 98 年,指考 91, 94 年)

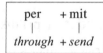

persist 〔 pɚ'sɪst 〕 v. 堅持

We have to *persist* to the last minute. (聯考 70, 79, 83 年,學測 94, 100, 101 年,指考 101 年)

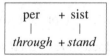

persuade 〔 pɚ'swed 〕 v. 說服

To talk someone into doing something is to *persuade* him to do it. (模考 91 年,聯考 54, 55, 66, 79, 86, 87, 88 年,學測 86, 87, 92 ②, 94, 97, 101 年,指考 92, 93 ②, 95, 96, 101, 102 年)

precede 〔 prɪ'sid 〕 *v.* 在～之前

Mr. Kennedy was *preceded* by Mr. Eisenhower as president. (聯考 64 年)

```
  pre   + cede          pre   + dict
   |       |             |       |
before +  go          before +  say
```

predict 〔 prɪ'dɪkt 〕 *v.* 預測

The weather bureau *predicted* that a typhoon was coming. (模考 83 年，聯考 63, 66, 71, 81, 87 年，學測 83, 88, 91 ①, 98 年，指考 92 年)

prescribe 〔 prɪ'skraɪb 〕 *v.* 開藥方

The doctor *prescribed* some painkillers for me. (聯考 55, 74, 87 年，學測 86, 94 年，指考 96 年)

```
  per   + scribe
   |       |
before +  write
```

present〔 prɪ'zɛnt 〕 v. 贈送

The students expressed their thanks to Prof. Davis by *presenting* him with a parting gift.

(聯考 62, 64, 65, 66, 68, 69, 70, 73, 76, 77, 78, 81, 84, 85, 86, 90 年，學測 84, 87, 88, 90, 92 ②, 100 年，指考 92, 93 ①, 95, 100, 102 年)

preserve〔 prɪ'zɝv 〕 v. 保存

The dry desert air has *preserved* the mummy.

(模考 83 年，聯考 68, 70, 79, 84 年，學測 96, 98, 99, 100 年，指考 94, 96, 100 年)

presume〔 prɪ'zum 〕 v. 推測

I *presume* from your accent that you are an Englishman. (模考 91 年，聯考 71 年)

pretend〔 prɪ'tɛnd 〕 v. 假裝

Mary didn't want to go to school, so she *pretended* that she was sick. (聯考 46, 51, 59, 68 年，學測 94, 97 年)

prohibit〔pro'hɪbɪt〕*v.* 禁止

Smoking is *prohibited* everywhere in this building. (聯考 80, 84 年,指考 93 ① 年)

promote〔prə'mot〕*v.* 促進

The mission of the former U.S. president was to *promote* peace. (模考 82 年,聯考 64, 76, 88, 84, 89, 90 年,學測 83, 86, 92 ①, 97, 98, 99, 101 年,指考 91, 92, 94, 96, 98, 99, 101 年)

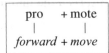 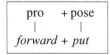

propose〔prə'poz〕*v.* 提議

We *proposed* a reform plan to the company, but it was turned down. (模考 91 年,聯考 63, 84, 88 年,學測 88, 91 ①, 100, 101 年,指考 93 ②, 94, 98 年)

purchase〔'pɝtʃəs〕*v.* 購買

You can *purchase* the tickets at the theaters' booking offices. (聯考 59, 78, 83 年,學測 92 ①, 93, 99, 102 年,指考 92, 93 ②, 98, 101 年)

自我測驗

- [ ] prescribe   _____
- [ ] preserve   _____
- [ ] originate   _____
- [ ] paralyze   _____
- [ ] participate   _____

- [ ] oppose   _____
- [ ] panic   _____
- [ ] persist   _____
- [ ] permit   _____
- [ ] promote   _____

- [ ] overcome   _____
- [ ] offend   _____
- [ ] perform   _____
- [ ] precede   _____
- [ ] prohibit   _____

Check List

1. 贈　送　　p _____present_____ t
2. 反　對　　o _____ e
3. 參　加　　p _____ e
4. 提　議　　p _____ e
5. 組　織　　o _____ e

6. 推　測　　p _____ e
7. 克　服　　o _____ e
8. 說　服　　p _____ e
9. 起　源　　o _____ e
10. 購　買　　p _____ e

11. 預　測　　p _____ t
12. 使麻痺　　p _____ e
13. 允　許　　p _____ t
14. 假　裝　　p _____ d
15. 堅　持　　p _____ t

pursue 〔 pɚˋsu 〕 v. 追求

You would have absolute freedom as to what research you thought it best to *pursue*.

(聯考 49, 67 年，學測 93, 100 年，指考 98 年)

Q q

qualify 〔ˋkwɑləˌfaɪ 〕 v. 使有資格

His skills *qualify* him for the job. (模考 91 年，

聯考 52, 66, 72, 73, 74, 75, 86 年，學測 88 年，指考 92, 93 ②, 94, 97, 98 年)

R r

recall 〔 rɪˋkɔl 〕 v. 想起

I *recall* having met the woman before.

(聯考 49, 64, 83, 88 年，學測 87, 88, 92 ②, 94, 102 年，指考 100 年)

recognize 〔ˋrɛkəgˌnaɪz 〕 v. 認出

He is unusually tall, so it is easy to *recognize* him in the crowd. (聯考 48, 67, 68, 72, 73, 81, 84, 85, 88, 90 年，

學測 85, 88, 91 ①, 92 ①, 93, 96, 97, 101, 102 年，指考 91, 93 ①②, 96, 99 年)

recommend 〔ˌrɛkəˈmɛnd 〕 *v.* 推薦

Can you *recommend* any good restaurant in the neighborhood? (模考 91 年，聯考 49, 52, 53, 80, 87, 88 年，學測 96, 99 年，指考 98, 99, 100 年)

refer 〔 rɪˈfɝ 〕 *v.* 參考

For additional explanation, please *refer* to page 20. (聯考 58, 62, 63, 69, 88, 89 年，學測 87, 92 ②, 93, 98, 99, 102 年，指考 91, 92, 93 ①, 95, 97, 98, 99, 100, 101, 102 年)

reflect 〔 rɪˈflɛkt 〕 *v.* 反映

Her face was *reflected* in the mirror. (聯考 48, 52, 81, 82, 86, 87, 89 年，學測 83 年，指考 91, 93 ①②, 97, 101 年)

re	+	flect
back	+	*bend*

regain 〔 rɪˈgen 〕 *v.* 恢復

After three hours, the patient *regained* consciousness. (聯考 82 年，學測 94 年，指考 91 年)

reject 〔 rɪ'dʒɛkt 〕 v. 拒絕

The government *rejected*
the plan to lower taxes.

(聯考 66, 74, 76 年，學測 83, 86, 92 ②, 94, 96 年，指考 99 年)

relieve 〔 rɪ'liv 〕 v. 減輕

The appointment of another doctor to help
me has *relieved* me of a lot of work.

(模考 91 年，聯考 45, 51, 61, 65, 73, 83, 84, 90 年，學測 88, 89, 91 ①, 92 ①, 94,
99, 101, 102 年，指考 93 ①, 100 年)

rely 〔 rɪ'laɪ 〕 v. 依賴

Children *rely* on their parents for love and
support. (聯考 46, 84, 90 年，學測 94, 102 年，指考 93 ①②, 96, 102 年)

remain 〔 rɪ'men 〕 v. 依然

The question *remains* to be solved. (模考 91 年，
聯考 47, 63, 65, 69, 74, 82, 84, 85, 87, 88, 90 年，學測 84, 88, 90, 91 ①, 92 ②, 93,
97, 99, 100 年，指考 95, 97, 98, 101, 102 年)

remark 〔 rɪˈmɑrk 〕 *v.* 評論

The guests present *remarked* on her dress.

(模考 91 年，聯考 49 年，學測 86 年，指考 93 ②, 99 年)

replace 〔 rɪˈples 〕 *v.* 取代

I *replaced* the worn-out tires with new ones.

(模考 82 年，聯考 63, 64, 75, 76, 86, 87 年，學測 84, 86, 92 ②, 94, 98, 99, 100, 101, 102 年，指考 92, 93 ②, 97, 99, 100, 101 年)

represent 〔ˌrɛprɪˈzɛnt 〕 *v.* 代表

The word "love" is often *represented* by a heart. (聯考 56, 65, 70, 78, 82, 88 年，學測 86, 88, 97, 101, 102 年，指考 92, 94, 96, 98, 99 年)

require 〔 rɪˈkwaɪr 〕 *v.* 需要

This project will *require* a lot of money and manpower. (模考 91 年，聯考 49, 54, 63, 64, 65, 69, 72, 74, 87, 90 年，學測 83, 85, 86, 87, 88, 90, 91 ②, 93, 99, 101, 102 年，指考 92, 93 ①②, 94, 97, 98, 100 年)

resemble〔rɪˈzɛmbḷ〕v. 相像

In his easy-going character, Jim seems to *resemble* his father. (模考 91 年，聯考 46, 48, 49, 53, 90 年，學測 85 年，指考 96, 102 年)

reserve〔rɪˈzɝv〕v. 預約

I'd like to *reserve* a table for two. (模考 83 年，聯考 57, 60, 67, 71, 81, 83, 88 年，學測 83, 91 ①②, 93, 102 年，指考 93 ②, 94, 98, 99 年)

resign〔rɪˈzaɪn〕v. 辭職

He *resigned* from the editorship of the school paper. (聯考 50, 82 年，學測 89, 96, 98 年，指考 97 年)

resist〔rɪˈzɪst〕v. 抗拒

Most children can't *resist* the temptation of ice cream, especially in summer. (聯考 47, 56, 63, 66, 68, 69, 71, 83, 87 年，學測 87, 91 ①, 92 ①, 94, 99, 100, 102 年，指考 96, 98, 101 年)

respond 〔 rɪ'spɑnd 〕 v. 回應

I offered to help him,
but he didn't *respond*.

re + spond
|　　　|
back + promise

(聯考 67, 69, 79, 81, 83, 85, 89, 90 年，學測 86,

88, 91 ②, 93, 96 年，指考 92, 93 ①②, 96, 98 年)

restore 〔 rɪ'stor 〕 v. 修復

They spent a large sum of money *restoring*
the ancient temple. (聯考 50, 72, 90 年，學測 90, 94 年，

指考 91, 94 年)

restrict 〔 rɪ'strɪkt 〕 v. 限制

This movie is *restricted* to adults only.

(聯考 67, 71, 73, 84 年，學測 89, 90, 102 年，指考 100 年)

resume 〔 rɪ'zum 〕 v. 恢復

Owing to the heavy storm, the flights won't
be *resumed* until next Tuesday. (模考 91 年，

聯考 73 年，學測 88 年)

自我測驗

- [ ] resume _____
- [ ] restore _____
- [ ] recall _____
- [ ] refer _____
- [ ] remain _____

- [ ] resemble _____
- [ ] resign _____
- [ ] replace _____
- [ ] qualify _____
- [ ] represent _____

- [ ] reject _____
- [ ] remark _____
- [ ] require _____
- [ ] pursue _____
- [ ] reflect _____

Check List

1. 恢　復　　r ___*regain*___ n
2. 取　代　　r _____ e
3. 回　應　　r _____ d
4. 抗　拒　　r _____ t
5. 修　復　　r _____ e

6. 認　出　　r _____ e
7. 反　映　　r _____ t
8. 代　表　　r _____ t
9. 預　約　　r _____ e
10. 依　賴　　r _____ y

11. 限　制　　r _____ t
12. 追　求　　p _____ e
13. 推　薦　　r _____ d
14. 減　輕　　r _____ e
15. 評　論　　r _____ k

retain 〔rɪˈten〕 *v.* 保留

My grandmother *retained* clear memories of her youth. (聯考 72, 74, 82, 87 年，學測 84, 97, 100 年，指考 97, 100 年)

retard 〔rɪˈtɑrd〕 *v.* 妨礙

Malnutrition will *retard* the growth of children. (模考 82 年)

retrieve 〔rɪˈtriv〕 *v.* 尋回

The policemen *retrieved* the luggage she had been robbed of three days later. (模考 91 年，聯考 54, 78 年，指考 97, 99 年)

re	+	trieve
again	+	*find*

reveal 〔rɪˈvil〕 *v.* 洩漏

Don't *reveal* that we saw them coming out of the store. (聯考 46, 62, 85, 88 年，學測 91 ②, 93, 96 年，指考 92, 93 ②, 94, 95, 99, 100, 101 年)

roar〔ror〕*v.* 吼叫

After making successive speeches, he *roared* himself hoarse. (聯考 46, 55, 60, 66, 75 年,

學測 91 ① 年)

S s

scatter〔'skætɚ〕*v.* 散布

He *scattered* crumbs for the pigeons on the square every day. (學測 98 年,指考 94, 98 年)

scream〔skrim〕*v.* 尖叫

I heard someone *screaming* when I happened to be passing through the village. (聯考 50 年,

學測 87, 97, 100 年,指考 94 年)

seize〔siz〕*v.* 抓住

He was eager to *seize* the opportunity.

(聯考 45, 54, 60, 68 年,學測 92 ②, 93, 102 年,指考 102 年)

separate〔'sɛpə,ret〕v. 區分

Children can't *separate* good from evil.

(聯考 64, 71, 78, 88, 90 年，學測 83, 86, 87, 96 年，指考 93 ①, 95, 102 年)

sharpen〔'ʃɑrpən〕v. 使銳利

If you want to become a good tennis player, you have to *sharpen* your skills. (聯考 45, 54, 56, 59, 67, 81 年，學測 92 ②, 97, 98, 99 年，指考 95 年)

shatter〔'ʃætɚ〕v. 破碎

My dreams have been *shattered* after successive failures. (聯考 51, 76 年)

slip〔slɪp〕v. 滑倒

He *slipped* on the icy road and sprained his ankle. (聯考 76 年，學測 93, 101 年，指考 92, 93 ①, 98, 102 年)

soar〔sor〕v. 高飛

Eagles look proud, especially when they *soar* high in the sky.

sparkle (ˈspɑrkḷ) *v.* 閃耀

The jewels on her were *sparkling* radiantly.

(學測 96, 99 年)

specialize (ˈspɛʃəlˌaɪz) *v.* 專攻

My uncle advised me to *specialize* in history. (聯考 52, 70 年)

splash (splæʃ) *v.* 濺起

Bending over the basin, he *splashed* cold water on his face.

stammer (ˈstæmɚ) *v.* 口吃

It is amazing that the eloquent politician should *stammer* when questioned about his marriage. (模考 91 年)

stimulate (ˈstɪmjəˌlet) *v.* 刺激

Praise and encouragement can *stimulate* a person to make further efforts, because it can inspire self-confidence. (聯考 88 年，指考 97 年)

strengthen (ˈstrɛŋθən) v. 加強

We are willing to *strengthen* our ties with those countries that are friendly to us. (聯考 49, 61, 66, 69, 74, 75, 83, 86 年，學測 84, 92 ②, 93, 98 年，指考 92, 93 ②, 97, 98, 100 年)

stress (strɛs) v. 強調

I have to *stress* the point that this is not a trial but an inquiry. (聯考 66, 73, 77, 89, 90 年，學測 92 ①, 97, 98 年，指考 98, 99, 100 年)

stretch (strɛtʃ) v. 伸展

After studying at the desk for hours, he went out of his room to *stretch* his legs. (聯考 66, 75 年，學測 88, 89, 91 ①②, 96, 99 年，指考 98, 100 年)

struggle (ˈstrʌgl̩) v. 掙扎

The trapped fox *struggled* violently to get free. (聯考 45, 50, 54 年，學測 87, 102 年，指考 92, 93 ①②, 102 年)

stumble 〔'stʌmbḷ 〕 *v.* 絆倒

While going upstairs, she *stumbled* and nearly fell. (模考 91 年，指考 97 年)

submit 〔 səb'mɪt 〕 *v.* 屈服

He *submitted* to the temptation and stole the wallet. (聯考 54 年，學測 87 年，指考 95 年)

```
sub  + mit
 |       |
under + send ( 從下面過去 )
```

subscribe 〔 səb'skraɪb 〕 *v.* 訂閱

What kind of magazine do you want to *subscribe* to? (模考 91 年)

substitute 〔'sʌbstə‚tjut 〕 *v.* 代替

We *substituted* a red ball for a blue one to see if the baby would notice the difference.

(聯考 50, 75, 76, 90 年，學測 90, 92 ①②, 96, 100 年，指考 93 ①, 94, 98 年)

- [ ] retrieve _____
- [ ] retard _____
- [ ] seize _____
- [ ] sparkle _____
- [ ] stammer _____

- [ ] stress _____
- [ ] submit _____
- [ ] shatter _____
- [ ] scream _____
- [ ] retain _____

- [ ] splash _____
- [ ] roar _____
- [ ] soar _____
- [ ] slip _____
- [ ] stretch _____

Check List

1. 散　布　　s ___*scatter*___ r
2. 洩　漏　　r _____ l
3. 區　分　　s _____ e
4. 專　攻　　s _____ e
5. 濺　起　　s _____ h

6. 伸　展　　s _____ h
7. 訂　閱　　s _____ e
8. 使銳利　　s _____ n
9. 刺　激　　s _____ e
10. 加　強　　s _____ n

11. 掙　扎　　s _____ e
12. 絆　倒　　s _____ e
13. 代　替　　s _____ e
14. 閃　耀　　s _____ e
15. 尋　回　　r _____ e

succeed〔səkˋsid〕 v. 繼承

He will *succeed* his father as president of
the company. (聯考 51, 66, 67, 68 年，

學測 84, 86, 87, 90, 91 ①, 94, 96 年，指考 92, 94,

97, 101, 102 年)

```
suc  + ceed
 |       |
under +  go
```

surrender〔səˋrɛndɚ〕 v. 投降

After being under siege for three months,
the army finally *surrendered*. (聯考 60, 72 年，

學測 102 年)

surround〔səˋraʊnd〕 v. 包圍

The castle was *surrounded* by high walls.

(聯考 47, 53, 69, 71 年，學測 91 ①, 99, 100, 101 年，指考 94, 100 年)

suspect〔səˋspɛkt〕 v. 懷疑

She *suspected* him of taking her money.

(聯考 59, 61, 64 年，學測 97, 102 年，指考 96 年)

suspend 〔 sə'spɛnd 〕 *v.* 暫停

The security guard will be *suspended* until the investigation is completed. (學測 89 年,

指考 97 年)

sustain 〔 sə'sten 〕 *v.* 支撐

The columns *sustain* the heavy roof of the building.

(聯考 85 年, 學測 92 ①, 100 年)

sus	+	tain
under	+	keep , hold

symbolize 〔'sɪmbḷ͵aɪz 〕 *v.* 象徵

Flowers are used to *symbolize* our feelings.

(模考 91 年,指考 99 年)

T t

threaten 〔'θrɛtṇ 〕 *v.* 威脅

The woman caught the boy stealing her money and *threatened* to call the police.

(聯考 63, 80 年,學測 85, 93, 94, 99, 101 年,指考 95, 96, 101, 102 年)

tolerate ('talə,ret) *v.* 忍受

I refuse to *tolerate* his actions any longer.

(聯考 49, 60, 64, 73, 80, 86, 88 年，學測 83, 88, 92 ①②, 97 年，指考 92 年)

trace (tres) *v.* 追溯

The custom can be *traced* back to the
fifteen century. (聯考 65 年，學測 87, 101 年)

transfer (træns'fɝ) *v.* 轉移

The head office has been
transferred from London
to Paris. (學測 92②, 96, 101, 102 年，

指考 94, 102 年)

trans	+	fer
across	+	carry

transform (træns'fɔrm) *v.* 改變

Experience and hardship have *transformed*
the proud boy into a humble man. (模考 82②，

學測 87, 96 年，指考 93①, 99, 100 年)

transmit 〔 træns′mɪt 〕 *v.* 傳達

He *transmitted* his ideas to other people
by lecturing. (聯考 70, 85 年)

transport 〔 træns′port 〕 *v.* 運輸

People use the river to *transport* goods.

(聯考 52, 53, 70, 80, 81, 82, 87 年,學測 88, 90, 97, 98 年,指考 92, 93 ②, 94 年)

twinkle 〔′twɪŋkl̩ 〕 *v.* 閃耀

The diamond on her finger was *twinkling*
in the light. (學測 89 年)

twist 〔 twɪst 〕 *v.* 扭傷

Jack fell down while playing tennis and
twisted his ankle badly. (聯考 84 年,學測 98, 101 年,

指考 100 年)

U u

urge (ɝdʒ) *v.* 力勸

Last night, in a TV address, the President
urged us to support the Red Cross.

(聯考 48, 65, 67, 87, 88 年,學測 85, 86, 92 ①, 94 年,指考 98 年)

V v

vanish ('vænɪʃ) *v.* 消失

With a wave of his hand, the magician
made the rabbit *vanish*. (聯考 59, 64, 81 年,學測 89 年)

violate ('vaɪə,let) *v.* 違反

Whoever *violates* the rule will be fined
500 dollars. (聯考 88 年,學測 83, 85, 100 年,指考 98 年)

W w

whisper ('hwɪspɚ) *v.* 低語

Stop *whispering* in the corner; say whatever
it is out loud. (聯考 48 年)

withdraw 〔 wɪθˋdrɔ 〕 *v.* 撤退

They determined to *withdraw* the troops from the front line. (聯考 56, 69, 70 年，學測 102 年)

witness 〔ˋwɪtnɪs 〕 *v.* 目睹

The traffic accident was *witnessed* by two high school students. (聯考 50, 66, 72, 83, 84 年，學測 99 年，指考 93 ② 年)

―― 【劉毅老師的話】 ――

動詞是一個句子的靈魂，背完了本單元 327 個動詞，你是否覺得功力大增、信心十足了呢？下一個階段是形容詞，能讓你造的句子更精采、更生動。加油，不要鬆懈。

自 我 測 驗

- [ ] surrender   _____
- [ ] sustain   _____
- [ ] tolerate   _____
- [ ] transform   _____
- [ ] twinkle   _____

- [ ] suspend   _____
- [ ] violate   _____
- [ ] witness   _____
- [ ] transfer   _____
- [ ] withdraw   _____

- [ ] vanish   _____
- [ ] surround   _____
- [ ] transmit   _____
- [ ] symbolize   _____
- [ ] threaten   _____

1. 繼　承　　s _____*succeed*_____ d

2. 懷　疑　　s _____ t

3. 運　輸　　t _____ t

4. 低　語　　w _____ r

5. 目　睹　　w _____ s

6. 撤　退　　w _____ w

7. 追　溯　　t _____ e

8. 扭　傷　　t _____ t

9. 消　失　　v _____ h

10. 閃　耀　　t _____ e

11. 象　徵　　s _____ e

12. 投　降　　s _____ r

13. 威　脅　　t _____ n

14. 力　勸　　u _____ e

15. 忍　受　　t _____ e

★ 形容詞

academic 〔‚ækə'dɛmɪk〕 *adj.* 學術的

They are now actively broadening *academic* exchanges between the two countries. (聯考 53, 70, 72 年，學測 99 年，指考 96, 98, 99, 100 年)

acceptable 〔 ək'sɛptəbḷ 〕 *adj.* 可接受的

He kindly offered me a suggestion, but I don't think it's *acceptable*. (聯考 47, 52, 54, 62, 66, 67, 68, 69, 71, 80, 83, 85, 88, 89 年，學測 85, 87, 88, 90, 92 ①②, 93, 94, 96, 99, 100, 101, 102 年，指考 95, 96, 97, 98, 100, 101 年)

accurate 〔'ækjərɪt〕 *adj.* 準確的

The watch my grandfather gave me still keeps *accurate* time. (聯考 63, 64, 67, 70, 71, 85 年，學測 93 年，指考 93 ①②, 95 年)

ac	+	cur	+	ate
to	+	care	+	*adj.*

accustomed (ə'kʌstəmd) *adj.* 習慣的

Many foreigners are not *accustomed* to the weather in Taiwan. (聯考 53, 83 年，學測 83, 84, 92 ②年，指考 93 ①年)

addicted (ə'dɪktɪd) *adj.* 沉溺於

More and more people have become *addicted* to smoking. (學測 91 ①年，指考 96, 98, 101 年)

additional (ə'dɪʃənl̩) *adj.* 額外的

The work cannot be finished this week. It will take an *additional* week. (聯考 73, 75, 80, 89, 90 年，學測 88, 91 ②, 99, 100, 101 年，指考 92, 93 ②, 94, 96, 97, 99, 100, 101 年)

adequate ('ædəkwɪt) *adj.* 足夠的

Are you getting an *adequate* wage for the work you are doing? (聯考 68, 69, 87 年)

admirable ('ædmərəbl̩) *adj.* 令人欽佩的

Their determination to fight to the last man was really *admirable*. (聯考 47, 68, 72, 74, 79, 84, 87, 88, 89 年，學測 86, 88, 90, 91 ②, 92 ①, 93, 94, 100 年，指考 102 年)

advanced 〔 əd'vænst 〕 *adj.* 高深的

He decided to go abroad for *advanced* studies.

(聯考 67, 68, 80, 88, 90 年，學測 90, 91 ②, 94, 98, 101 年，指考 93 ②, 94, 97, 100 年)

aggressive 〔 ə'grɛsɪv 〕 *adj.* 有攻擊性的

Be careful. When startled, even a tamed animal can become very *aggressive*.

(模考 91 年，聯考 47, 72, 73, 79 年，學測 88, 100 年，指考 93 ①, 96, 101 年)

alphabetical 〔 ˌælfə'bɛtɪkl̩ 〕 *adj.* 按字母序的

The words in an English dictionary are arranged in *alphabetical* order. (聯考 53, 82 年)

```
alpha + bet(a) + ical
  |        |        |
  α    +   β    +  adj.
 (α和β即希臘字母的 A 和 B )
```

ambiguous 〔 æm'bɪgjʊəs 〕 *adj.* 模稜兩可的

The sentence written on the board is *ambiguous*. It has more than one meaning.

(模考 91 年，學測 88 年)

ambitious〔æmˈbɪʃəs〕*adj.* 有抱負的

John wants to be an outstanding physicist.
He is an *ambitious* young man. (聯考 52, 65, 68, 79,

87 年，學測 86, 92 ② 年，指考 93 ①, 100 年)

anonymous〔əˈnɑnəməs〕*adj.* 匿名的

The incident was exposed by an *anonymous*
letter sent to the newspaper. (學測 86, 89 年)

an	+ onym	+ ous
without	+ *name*	+ *adj.*

anxious〔ˈæŋkʃəs〕*adj.* 焦急的

An *anxious* crowd waited outside the
building for the results of the election.

(聯考 50, 61, 65, 74, 76, 89, 90 年，學測 91 ①, 98, 99, 100 年，指考 92, 96 年)

appropriate〔əˈproprɪɪt〕*adj.* 適當的

Sports wear is not *appropriate* for such a
formal occasion. (學測 88, 97, 98 年，指考 94, 95, 96 年)

arrogant 〔'ærəgənt 〕 *adj.* 自大的

Some people are too *arrogant* to ask questions; they consider it beneath their dignity. (模考 91 年，指考 92 年)

artificial 〔ˌɑrtə'fɪʃəl 〕 *adj.* 人造的

I don't like *artificial* flowers, for they can't give forth fragrance. (聯考 49, 85 年，學測 87, 93, 100 年，指考 93 ①, 94, 97 年)

available 〔 ə'veləbḷ 〕 *adj.* 可得的

Airline tickets are not easily *available* because of the coming New Year holidays. (聯考 65, 71, 72, 89 年，學測 88, 93, 94, 96, 97, 99, 102 年，指考 92, 94, 96, 97, 98 年)

average 〔'ævərɪdʒ 〕 *adj.* 平均的

The *average* age of the boys in this class is sixteen. (聯考 60, 61, 66, 67, 70, 73, 76, 80, 83, 84, 85, 87 年，學測 89, 92 ②, 98, 100, 102 年，指考 92, 93 ①, 95, 97, 98, 99, 102 年)

B b

bankrupt 〔'bæŋkrʌpt 〕 *adj.* 破產的

The recession has made many small companies go *bankrupt*. (模考 91 年，學測 92 ① 年，

指考 92, 96 年)

bare 〔 bɛr 〕 *adj.* 赤裸的

A girl with long straight hair roamed on the beach in her *bare* feet. (聯考 56, 65, 67, 84 年，學測 92 ②, 99 年)

beneficial 〔ˌbɛnə'fɪʃəl 〕 *adj.* 有益的

Taking exercise every day is absolutely *beneficial* for your health. (聯考 46, 67, 85, 87, 89, 90 年，

學測 87, 88, 90, 91 ①, 92 ① ②, 96, 97, 98, 100 年)

bene	+	fic	+ ial
good	+	make	+ adj.

brief 〔 brif 〕 *adj.* 簡短的

He made a *brief* statement after the meeting.

(聯考 51, 67, 79, 82, 88 年，學測 86, 91 ②, 100 年，指考 102 年)

自 我 測 驗

- [ ] addicted _____
- [ ] ambiguous _____
- [ ] artificial _____
- [ ] brief _____
- [ ] average _____

- [ ] bare _____
- [ ] alphabetical _____
- [ ] bankrupt _____
- [ ] beneficial _____
- [ ] acceptable _____

- [ ] additional _____
- [ ] ambitious _____
- [ ] aggressive _____
- [ ] available _____
- [ ] admirable _____

Check List

1. 焦急的   a ___*anxious*___ s
2. 學術的   a _____ c
3. 高深的   a _____ d
4. 有益的   b _____ l
5. 平均的   a _____ e
6. 習慣的   a _____ d
7. 足夠的   a _____ e
8. 自大的   a _____ t
9. 人造的   a _____ l
10. 破產的   b _____ t
11. 準確的   a _____ e
12. 額外的   a _____ l
13. 匿名的   a _____ s
14. 適當的   a _____ e
15. 簡短的   b _____ f

C c

capable 〔ˈkepəbḷ 〕 *adj.* 有能力的

Mr. Peterson is *capable* of finishing the job alone. (聯考 50, 64, 71, 79, 86 年，學測 88, 91 ①, 97, 101 年，指考 97 年)

cautious 〔ˈkɔʃəs 〕 *adj.* 小心的

You must be very *cautious* when crossing the street. (聯考 49, 63, 65, 67, 71 年，學測 86, 90 年，指考 93 ①, 96, 98 年)

characteristic 〔͵kærɪktəˈrɪstɪk 〕 *adj.* 獨特的

Tom is shy, and it is *characteristic* of him to speak as little as possible. (聯考 52, 60, 73, 90 年，指考 91, 96, 100 年)

cheerful 〔ˈtʃɪrfəl 〕 *adj.* 愉快的

Chris has a *cheerful* personality. Everyone likes to be with him. (聯考 49, 56, 65, 66, 74, 75, 83, 86 年，學測 86 年，指考 101 年)

competent 〔'kɑmpətənt 〕 *adj.* 能幹的

Mr. Wilson is *competent* enough to do the work by himself. (模考 82 年，聯考 75 年，指考 96 年)

complex 〔 kəm'plɛks 〕 *adj.* 複雜的

The problem is too *complex* for them to understand. (聯考 51, 64, 65, 67, 78 年，指考 93 ①, 95, 97, 99 年)

complicated 〔'kɑmplə,ketɪd 〕 *adj.* 複雜的

That puzzle is too *complicated* for the children. (模考 83 年，聯考 64, 76, 80, 82 年，學測 83, 85, 91 ②年，指考 94, 95, 97 年)

concrete 〔'kɑnkrit 〕 *adj.* 具體的

George seems to have some *concrete* ideas on how to handle the problem.

(聯考 85 年，學測 98, 102 年，指考 94, 99, 101, 102 年)

conscious〔ˈkɑnʃəs〕*adj.* 有意識的

He was *conscious* that he was being followed. (模考 83 年，聯考 45, 83, 90 年，學測 91 ①, 92 ①②, 94, 101 年，指考 95, 96, 97 年)

conservative〔kənˈsɝvətɪv〕*adj.* 保守的

My grandmother is very *conservative*. She doesn't allow girls to wear miniskirts.

(學測 91 ①, 92 ② 年)

considerable〔kənˈsɪdərəbl̩〕*adj.* 相當大的

Due to the fall of the stocks, he lost a *considerable* sum of money. (模考 91 年，聯考 49, 72, 79, 80 年，學測 90, 101, 102 年，指考 93 ② 年)

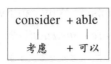

```
consider + able
   |         |
  考慮    + 可以
```

considerate〔kənˈsɪdərɪt〕*adj.* 體貼的

All the patients like Mary. She is always *considerate*. (聯考 49, 69, 79, 85, 90 年，學測 87, 92 ②, 100 年，指考 91, 97 年)

```
consider  +  ate
   |          |
  考慮    +  adj.（為別人考慮的）
```

constant〔ˈkɑnstənt〕*adj.* 不變的

The scar on her face is a *constant* reminder of the accident. (聯考 48, 51, 54, 63, 67, 68, 79, 82, 89 年，學測 83, 88, 92 ①②, 98, 101, 102 年，指考 94, 96, 99, 102 年)

constructive〔kənˈstrʌktɪv〕*adj.* 有建設性的

For hours, we have heard nothing but negative criticism. Why can't you say something more *constructive*? (聯考 66, 73, 80, 84, 87 年，學測 86, 94, 96, 97 年，指考 91, 92, 93 ②, 94, 101, 102 年)

contagious〔kən'tedʒəs〕*adj.* 傳染性的

Be careful; the disease is highly *contagious*.

(模考 91 年，聯考 81 年，指考 93 ① 年)

contaminated〔kən'tæmə,netɪd〕*adj.*
受到污染的

It was said that many people had died from
drinking *contaminated* water. (模考 91 年，指考 102 年)

controversial〔,kɑntrə'vɝʃəl〕*adj.*
有爭議性的

The building of the fourth nuclear power
plant is a *controversial* issue in Taiwan.

(模考 91 年，聯考 50 年，學測 87 年，指考 102 年)

corrupt〔kə'rʌpt〕*adj.* 腐敗的

The *corrupt* government
was overthrown in a
revolution. (模考 91 年，聯考 71 年)

cor + rupt
| |
all + break

countless 〔'kauntlɪs 〕 *adj.* 無數的

There are *countless* stars and galaxies in the universe. (學測 100 年，指考 100 年)

courteous 〔'kɝtɪəs 〕 *adj.* 有禮貌的

The salesman's *courteous* attitude has softened the anger of the customer. (模考 91 年，聯考 83 年，學測 85, 89, 92 ②年，指考 96 年)

critical 〔'krɪtɪkl̩ 〕 *adj.* 危急的

The patient is in *critical* condition; he needs immediate surgery. (聯考 85 年，指考 99, 100 年)

cunning 〔'kʌnɪŋ 〕 *adj.* 狡猾的

The thief was very *cunning* and fooled the guard into letting him in. (聯考 90 年)

customary 〔'kʌstəm‚ɛrɪ 〕 *adj.* 習慣性的

Today, it is *customary* for people to shake hands upon meeting. (聯考 49, 51, 60 年，學測 88, 89, 93, 102 年，指考 91, 98, 102 年)

- [ ] concrete　　　＿＿＿＿＿＿＿＿＿
- [ ] considerable　　＿＿＿＿＿＿＿＿＿
- [ ] contaminated　　＿＿＿＿＿＿＿＿＿
- [ ] constructive　　＿＿＿＿＿＿＿＿＿
- [ ] countless　　　＿＿＿＿＿＿＿＿＿

- [ ] capable　　　　＿＿＿＿＿＿＿＿＿
- [ ] conscious　　　＿＿＿＿＿＿＿＿＿
- [ ] contagious　　　＿＿＿＿＿＿＿＿＿
- [ ] customary　　　＿＿＿＿＿＿＿＿＿
- [ ] courteous　　　＿＿＿＿＿＿＿＿＿

- [ ] controversial　　＿＿＿＿＿＿＿＿＿
- [ ] complex　　　　＿＿＿＿＿＿＿＿＿
- [ ] cheerful　　　　＿＿＿＿＿＿＿＿＿
- [ ] cunning　　　　＿＿＿＿＿＿＿＿＿
- [ ] constant　　　　＿＿＿＿＿＿＿＿＿

Check List

1. 腐敗的　　　c ___*corrupt*___ t
2. 小心的　　　c _____ s
3. 傳染性的　　c _____ s
4. 危急的　　　c _____ l
5. 體貼的　　　c _____ e

6. 複雜的　　　c _____ d
7. 能幹的　　　c _____ t
8. 保守的　　　c _____ e
9. 有意識的　　c _____ s
10. 不變的　　　c _____ t

11. 具體的　　　c _____ e
12. 獨特的　　　c _____ c
13. 愉快的　　　c _____ l
14. 無數的　　　c _____ s
15. 狡猾的　　　c _____ g

D d

decent 〔ˈdisṇt〕 *adj.* 合宜的

Jane pays attention to her appearance. She always wears *decent* clothes. (聯考 59, 67 年)

deceptive 〔dɪˈsɛptɪv〕 *adj.* 欺騙的

Don't judge a person by his appearance only, because appearances are often *deceptive*.

(學測 92 ① 年)

deficient 〔dɪˈfɪʃənt〕 *adj.* 不足的

I have faith in his ability; he is just *deficient* in courage.

(聯考 87, 88 年，指考 96 年)

de	+ fic	+ ient
down	+ make	+ adj.

definite 〔ˈdɛfənɪt〕 *adj.* 明確的

We cannot give you a *definite* answer now; there are still many uncertainties on this issue.

(聯考 48, 55, 72, 73, 83, 89, 90 年，學測 85, 87, 90, 92 ①, 94 年，指考 92, 94, 98 年)

democratic 〔͵dɛmə'krætɪk 〕 *adj.* 民主的

The manager is very *democratic* toward his fellow workers; he accepts constructive criticism. (聯考 86 年，指考 93 ②, 96 年)

dependent 〔 dɪ'pɛndənt 〕 *adj.* 依賴的

An illness during his childhood made him very *dependent* on his parents. (聯考 46, 51, 53, 69, 71, 76 年，學測 88, 92 ②, 94, 96, 101, 102 年，指考 96, 98, 99 年)

desperate 〔'dɛspərɪt 〕 *adj.* 絕望的

After her son's death, she felt *desperate*.

(聯考 90 年，指考 93 ①年)

destructive 〔 dɪ'strʌktɪv 〕 *adj.* 破壞性的

Nuclear weapons are so *destructive* that they shouldn't be developed. (模考 91 年，聯考 48, 67, 71, 85, 87, 90 年，學測 89, 97, 102 年，指考 91, 93 ①, 101 年)

detective 〔 dɪ'tɛktɪv 〕 *adj.* 偵探的

Old Professor Jones spends his time reading nothing but *detective* stories. (聯考 49, 65, 84 年，學測 85, 90, 96, 100, 102 年，指考 91, 92, 93 ①, 100, 101 年)

determined 〔 dɪ'tɝmɪnd 〕 *adj.* 堅決的

People who are *determined* cannot be easily stopped from doing what they want to do. (聯考 47, 53, 69, 71, 77, 84, 86, 88 年，學測 85, 86, 90, 91 ②, 92 ②, 96, 102 年，指考 91, 101 年)

direct 〔 də'rɛkt 〕 *adj.* 直接的

The foundation of all knowledge is our own *direct* personal experience. (聯考 83, 87, 90 年，學測 86, 88, 91 ②, 94, 96, 98, 99, 100, 101 年，指考 91, 92, 93 ②, 94, 97, 98, 99, 101, 102 年)

disastrous 〔 dɪz'æstrəs 〕 *adj.* 悲慘的

What had caused the *disastrous* accident was a mystery. (聯考 78 年，學測 86, 91 ①, 92 ①, 94, 97, 98, 99 年)

disgusting 〔 dɪs'gʌstɪŋ 〕 *adj.* 噁心的

The smell is *disgusting*. I feel like throwing
up. (模考 91 年,聯考 79 年,學測 99 年,指考 100 年)

disposable 〔 dɪ'spozəbḷ 〕 *adj.* 用完即丟的

Using *disposable* cups is convenient;
however, it produces more trash. (聯考 84 年,
學測 86, 92 ②年)

```
dis   + pos + able
 |       |      |
apart + put + 可以
```

distant 〔'dɪstənt 〕 *adj.* 遙遠的

The sun is *distant* from the earth. (聯考 66, 81, 82,
83 年,學測 91 ①②年)

disturbing 〔 dɪ'stɝbɪŋ 〕 *adj.* 令人不安的

The economic crisis we are having in Asia
now is very *disturbing* to many of us. (聯考 61,
64, 69, 78, 87, 90 年,學測 83, 87, 94 年)

divine 〔 də'vaɪn 〕 *adj.* 神聖的

To err is human, to forgive *divine*.

doubtful 〔'daʊtfəl 〕 *adj.* 懷疑的

Because Mr. Chang is always busy, it's *doubtful* whether he will come to the party.

(聯考 61, 67, 79, 87, 89 年，學測 83, 89, 90, 91 ① , 96 年，指考 93 ② 年)

drastic 〔'dræstɪk 〕 *adj.* 激烈的

Their *drastic* measures met with much protest from the crowd. (學測 89 年，指考 99 年)

dreadful 〔'drɛdfəl 〕 *adj.* 可怕的

Death is *dreadful* to everyone. (模考 83 年，

聯考 60 年，學測 89, 94, 99 年，指考 96 年)

E e

eager 〔'igɚ 〕 *adj.* 渴望的

He is *eager* to succeed and so he works very hard. (聯考 60, 64, 88 年，學測 88 年，指考 93 ① 年)

earnest 〔'ɝnɪst 〕 *adj.* 認真的

He told me in *earnest* that he would do everything to help me. (聯考 85, 89 年)

eccentric 〔 ɪk'sɛntrɪk 〕 *adj.* 古怪的

Mrs. Jackson is a very *eccentric* old woman. (指考 93①年)

```
ec  + centr  + ic
 |      |       |
out + center + adj. ( 偏離中心的 )
```

economical 〔ˌikə'nɑmɪkḷ 〕 *adj.* 節省的

An efficient engine is *economical* of fuel.

(聯考 63, 64, 76 年，學測 84 年)

edible 〔'ɛdəbḷ 〕 *adj.* 可食的

In fact, various parts of the lotus are *edible*.

(聯考 71 年，指考 100 年)

自我測驗

- ☐ disturbing _____
- ☐ eccentric _____
- ☐ disposable _____
- ☐ direct _____
- ☐ destructive _____

- ☐ definite _____
- ☐ deficient _____
- ☐ distant _____
- ☐ divine _____
- ☐ eager _____

- ☐ edible _____
- ☐ dependent _____
- ☐ drastic _____
- ☐ earnest _____
- ☐ dreadful _____

Check List

1. 偵探的   d *detective* e
2. 民主的   d _____ c
3. 堅決的   d _____ d
4. 可怕的   d _____ l
5. 節省的   e _____ l

6. 欺騙的   d _____ e
7. 噁心的   d _____ g
8. 絕望的   d _____ e
9. 悲慘的   d _____ s
10. 懷疑的   d _____ l

11. 古怪的   e _____ c
12. 合宜的   d _____ t
13. 激烈的   d _____ c
14. 可食的   e _____ e
15. 神聖的   d _____ e

effective 〔 ɪˈfɛktɪv 〕 *adj.* 有效的

Swimming is an *effective* way to achieve good health. (聯考 48, 63, 67, 68, 70, 71, 72, 80, 81, 83, 84, 88, 90 年，學測 83, 85, 87, 92 ①②, 93, 96, 97, 98, 99, 101 年，指考 91, 92, 93 ①②, 94, 95, 96, 98, 99, 100, 102 年)

```
ef  + fect  + ive
|      |       |
out + make  + adj.
```

efficient 〔 əˈfɪʃənt 〕 *adj.* 有效率的

Cars in the future will be characterized by their *efficient* use of gasoline. (聯考 48, 49, 60, 67, 69, 71, 78, 84, 86, 88, 89, 90 年，學測 85, 88, 91 ①, 94, 101 年，指考 95, 97 年)

elegant 〔 ˈɛləgənt 〕 *adj.* 優雅的

Miss White is an *elegant* and refined lady. (學測 88, 90 年)

elementary 〔 ˌɛləˈmɛntərɪ 〕 *adj.* 基本的

Elementary education is very important to the development of one's character. (模考 83 年，聯考 60, 74, 88 年，學測 83, 92 ①, 97, 99 年，指考 97, 98, 99 年)

eloquent 〔ˈɛləkwənt〕 *adj.* 雄辯的

The *eloquent* speaker convinces us all of the fact that no one is perfect. (模考 82, 91 年，學測 88 年，指考 93 ①, 94 年)

emotional 〔ɪˈmoʃənḷ〕 *adj.* 感情的

Sarah delivered an *emotional* appeal to the court and asked for mercy. (聯考 79, 87, 88, 89 年，學測 88, 91 ②, 96, 97, 100 年，指考 93 ①, 97, 98, 100, 102 年)

empty 〔ˈɛmptɪ〕 *adj.* 空的

The birds had gone and their nest was left *empty*. (聯考 79 年，學測 88, 92 ② 年，指考 91 年)

（p.250〜326）

endangered 〔ɪnˈdendʒɚd〕 *adj.* 瀕臨絕種的

It's time for us to make every effort to protect *endangered* species of animals. (聯考 85, 87 年，學測 94, 96, 99, 102 年)

```
en + danger + ed
 |      |      |
in + danger + adj.
```

enthusiastic 〔 ɪn͵θjuzɪˈæstɪk 〕 *adj.* 熱衷的

She is an *enthusiastic* admirer of the film
star. (聯考 47, 53, 66, 90 年，學測 83, 88, 91 ② 年，指考 91, 93 ①, 94, 95 年)

entire 〔 ɪnˈtaɪr 〕 *adj.* 全部的

We spent an *entire* day on the beach and
had a great time. (聯考 52, 59, 68, 70, 80, 84, 86, 87 年，學測 84,
92 ②, 97, 101, 102 年，指考 93 ②, 96, 98, 99 年)

equivalent 〔 ɪˈkwɪvələnt 〕 *adj.* 相等的

One U.S. dollar is *equivalent* to 33 New
Taiwan dollars. (聯考 85 年)

```
equi  +  val   + ent
  |        |      |
equal + worth + adj.
```

essential 〔 əˈsɛnʃəl 〕 *adj.* 必要的

Exercise, fresh air, and good food are
essential to health. (模考 91 年，聯考 49, 54, 68, 72, 87 年，
學測 86, 92 ②, 96, 99, 100, 102 年，指考 99 年)

evident 〔ˈɛvədənt 〕 *adj.* 明顯的

It's *evident* that moths are attracted to light.

(聯考 59 年，學測 94 年，指考 91 年)

excessive 〔 ɪkˈsɛsɪv 〕 *adj.* 過度的

This typhoon brought *excessive* rainfall and caused serious floods.

ex	+ cess	+ ive
out	+ *go*	+ *adj.*

(聯考 88 年，學測 99 年，指考 102 年)

exclusive 〔 ɪkˈsklusɪv 〕 *adj.* 獨占的

The TV station obtained the *exclusive* right to televise the match. (模考 91 年，聯考 49 年，指考 93 ①, 95, 96 年)

executive 〔 ɪgˈzɛkjutɪv 〕 *adj.* 執行的

An *executive* committee was set up and ten members were chosen. (學測 91 ②, 96 年，指考 98, 102 年)

explicit 〔 ɪkˈsplɪsɪt 〕 *adj.* 明確的

He made his instruction *explicit* and direct, so everyone could follow it easily. (聯考 71 年，學測 89, 92 ②, 98 年)

extensive 〔 ɪk'stɛnsɪv 〕 *adj.* 廣泛的

Dr. Smith acquired *extensive* knowledge
by reading various kinds of books. (模考 91 年,

聯考 51, 81, 82, 86 年,學測 86, 87, 92②, 94, 96 年,指考 94, 97, 98 年)

```
ex  +  tens  + ive
 |        |       |
out + stretch + adj.
```

extinct 〔 ɪk'stɪŋkt 〕 *adj.* 絕種的

If we don't act now, many rare animals
will become *extinct* soon. (聯考 71 年,學測 88 年,

指考 93②, 96 年)

extravagant 〔 ɪk'strævəgənt 〕 *adj.*
浪費的

She spent $10,000 buying a coat; it was
really an *extravagant* deed for a child to
do so. (模考 83 年,聯考 63 年)

F f

facial (ˈfeʃəl) *adj.* 臉的

A smile is a *facial* expression. (聯考 65, 66, 69, 79, 84, 90 年，學測 83, 89, 92②, 93, 100, 101, 102 年，指考 93②, 94, 97, 99, 100 年)

faint (fent) *adj.* 模糊的

I haven't the *faintest* idea as to what you mean. (學測 86 年)

fake (fek) *adj.* 仿冒的

He used *fake* money to make purchases and was caught by the police. (指考 94 年)

familiar (fəˈmɪljɚ) *adj.* 熟悉的

His face looks *familiar* to me, but I can't remember where I met him.

(聯考 61, 64, 66, 83, 89 年，學測 93, 94, 95, 96, 98, 101 年，指考 91, 94, 95, 100 年)

famili + ar
| |
family + adj.

自 我 測 驗

- [ ] endangered _____
- [ ] empty _____
- [ ] entire _____
- [ ] efficient _____
- [ ] excessive _____

- [ ] fake _____
- [ ] evident _____
- [ ] faint _____
- [ ] extravagant _____
- [ ] elegant _____

- [ ] extinct _____
- [ ] facial _____
- [ ] explicit _____
- [ ] essential _____
- [ ] extensive _____

Check List

1. 熟悉的　f ___*familiar*___ r

2. 浪費的　e _____ t

3. 過度的　e _____ e

4. 相等的　e _____ t

5. 執行的　e _____ e

6. 熱衷的　e _____ c

7. 雄辯的　e _____ t

8. 有效的　e _____ e

9. 優雅的　e _____ t

10. 基本的　e _____ y

11. 感情的　e _____ l

12. 明確的　e _____ t

13. 獨占的　e _____ e

14. 必要的　e _____ l

15. 模糊的　f _____ t

fancy (ˈfænsɪ) *adj.* 高級的

Mr. Williams is very rich, so he often takes his girlfriend to *fancy* restaurants. (聯考 67, 70 年，學測 101 年，指考 91 年)

fantastic (fænˈtæstɪk) *adj.* 極好的

I will never forget the *fantastic* night view of the bay. (聯考 78, 83 年，學測 91 ①, 92 ②年，指考 91, 100 年)

faulty (ˈfɔltɪ) *adj.* 錯誤的

Sorry for being late. Someone gave me *faulty* directions and I got totally lost. (聯考 61, 63, 68 年，學測 85 年，指考 94, 101 年)

favorable (ˈfevərəbḷ) *adj.* 有利的

The weather is *favorable* for an outing. (學測 90, 92 ①年，指考 101, 102 年)

feasible (ˈfizəbḷ) *adj.* 可行的

The company decided to put the plan into operation because it was the most *feasible* one. (聯考 89 年，指考 92 年)

fertile (ˈfɝtḷ) *adj.* 肥沃的

They plan to irrigate the desert areas and make them *fertile*. (模考 83 年)

fierce (fɪrs) *adj.* 激烈的

Since the contestants were all very good, the competition was *fierce*. (聯考 46, 84, 89 年，學測 92 ② 年，指考 91 年)

financial (fəˈnænʃəl) *adj.* 財務的

The merchant is in great *financial* difficulty because he has lost all his money. (聯考 47, 56, 61, 65, 82 年，學測 84, 88, 91 ①, 102 年，指考 91, 96, 100, 102 年)

flexible (ˈflɛksəbḷ) *adj.* 有彈性的

A *flexible* person does not insist on his own opinion and usually gets along with others well. (聯考 67, 71, 79, 86 年，學測 88, 92 ②, 98 年，指考 91, 98 年)

fluent 〔'fluənt 〕 *adj.* 流利的

American as she is, she can speak *fluent* Chinese.

(聯考 49, 85 年，學測 91 ① 年，指考 98 年)

```
flu   + ent
 |      |
flow  + adj.
```

formal 〔'fɔrml̩ 〕 *adj.* 正式的

A promise made by word of mouth is supposed to be as binding as a *formal* contract. (聯考 50, 83, 84, 88 年，學測 87, 90, 91 ①, 92 ①, 99, 101 年)

fragile 〔'frædʒəl 〕 *adj.* 脆弱的

Be careful of the vase; it is very *fragile*.

frightened 〔'fraɪtn̩d 〕 *adj.* 受驚的

The little girl was *frightened* at the sight of the big dog. (聯考 60, 62, 69, 74, 77, 78, 82, 90 年，學測 88, 91 ①, 100 年)

fundamental 〔ˌfʌndə'mɛntl̩ 〕 *adj.* 基本的

Freedom from fear should be a *fundamental* right of people of a country. (模考 83 年，聯考 90 年，指考 97, 101 年)

furnished (ˈfɝnɪʃt) *adj.* 有家具的

A room which has no furniture in it is not *furnished*. (聯考 52, 53, 55, 56, 62, 85, 90 年，學測 86, 92 ②年，指考 93 年)

G g

generous (ˈdʒɛnərəs) *adj.* 慷慨的

It is *generous* of him to give a large sum of money to the charity. (聯考 56, 61, 63, 82, 85, 89 年，學測 83, 86, 88, 90, 96, 97 年，指考 92 年)

genuine (ˈdʒɛnjʊɪn) *adj.* 真正的

This belt is made of *genuine* leather. (聯考 69, 71 年)

graceful (ˈgresfəl) *adj.* 優雅的

The ballet dancers' *graceful* movements delighted all the audience. (學測 90 年，指考 91 年)

grateful (ˈgretfəl) *adj.* 感激的

We are particularly *grateful* to him for his timely help. (聯考 74, 82, 87 年，學測 86, 97 年，指考 98 年)

guilty (ˈgɪltɪ) *adj.* 有罪的

The accused claimed that he was not *guilty* of the crime. (聯考 54, 59, 66, 67, 68 年，指考 91, 99 年)

H h

harmonious (harˈmonɪəs) *adj.* 和諧的

I like the picture; it has a *harmonious* arrangement of colors. (聯考 87, 88 年)

harsh (harʃ) *adj.* 嚴厲的

Mr. Jackson is a *harsh* and demanding teacher. (學測 87, 90, 102 年)

hasty (ˈhestɪ) *adj.* 匆促的

We should always keep in mind that *hasty* decisions often lead to regrets. (聯考 88 年)

honorable (ˈɑnərəbḷ) *adj.* 光榮的

His *honorable* deed in the war earned him a medal. (聯考 82, 84 年，學測 83, 88, 96, 97 年，指考 92, 93 ①, 94, 99, 101 年)

I i

identical 〔 aɪˈdɛntɪkḷ 〕 *adj.* 完全相同的

The study of the characteristics of these two plants shows that they are *identical* only in appearance. (聯考 90 年，學測 91 ①年，指考 93 ②, 95, 102 年)

ignorant 〔ˈɪgnərənt 〕 *adj.* 無知的

He is such a superficial and *ignorant* fellow.

(模考 82 年，聯考 54, 62, 66, 68, 69, 73, 79, 86, 87, 89 年，學測 87, 91 ①②, 92 ①, 94, 96, 101 年，指考 92, 93 ②, 95, 99, 100, 101 年)

illegal 〔 ɪˈligḷ 〕 *adj.* 非法的

It is *illegal* for any private citizen of our country to own a gun. (聯考 69, 78, 80, 87 年，指考 93 ②, 96, 98 年)

imaginary 〔 ɪˈmædʒəˌnɛrɪ 〕 *adj.* 想像的

The Tropic of Cancer is an *imaginary* line.

(聯考 56, 80, 81, 84, 86 年，學測 90, 91 ①②, 94, 98, 99 年，指考 94, 95 年)

- ☐ guilty _____
- ☐ hasty _____
- ☐ illegal _____
- ☐ fancy _____
- ☐ flexible _____

- ☐ favorable _____
- ☐ identical _____
- ☐ grateful _____
- ☐ fragile _____
- ☐ fluent _____

- ☐ formal _____
- ☐ faulty _____
- ☐ harsh _____
- ☐ genuine _____
- ☐ ignorant _____

1. 肥沃的　　f ___fertile___ e
2. 可行的　　f _____ e
3. 想像的　　i _____ y
4. 光榮的　　h _____ e
5. 優雅的　　g _____ l
6. 慷慨的　　g _____ s
7. 受驚的　　f _____ d
8. 基本的　　f _____ l
9. 激烈的　　f _____ e
10. 財務的　　f _____ l
11. 和諧的　　h _____ s
12. 有家具的　f _____ d
13. 眞正的　　g _____ e
14. 極好的　　f _____ c
15. 脆弱的　　f _____ e

imaginative 〔 ɪ'mædʒəˌnetɪv 〕 *adj.*
有想像力的

This scientist is very *imaginative*. His
original experiments are widely admired.

(模考 91 年，聯考 49, 67, 68, 69, 70, 81, 86, 87, 84, 88, 90 年，學測 90, 91 ②,
93 年，指考 91, 96, 97, 100 年)

impartial 〔 ɪm'parʃəl 〕 *adj.* 公平的

A judge should be *impartial*.

impatient 〔 ɪm'peʃənt 〕 *adj.* 不耐煩的

Don't be *impatient*. The train will arrive
in five minutes.   (聯考 86, 89 年，學測 84 年，指考 93 ②, 95 年)

impressive 〔 ɪm'prɛsɪv 〕 *adj.*
令人印象深刻的

His speech was very *impressive* and
thought-provoking.   (聯考 62, 66, 69, 73, 79, 84, 86, 88 年，
學測 84, 88, 91 ①, 92 ①, 94, 98, 101 年，指考 94 年)

inadequate 〔 ɪn'ædəkwɪt 〕 *adj.* 不足的

Mr. Wang's wage is *inadequate* for supporting the whole family. (學測 89 年)

incompatible 〔ˌɪnkəm'pætəbl̩ 〕 *adj.* 不合的

People said that the personalities of the young couple were *incompatible*.

incomprehensible 〔ˌɪnkɑmprɪ'hɛnsəbl̩ 〕 *adj.* 無法理解的

The lecture is Greek to me; in other words, it is *incomprehensible* to me. (指考 102 年)

incredible 〔 ɪn'krɛdəbl̩ 〕 *adj.* 難以置信的

It is *incredible* that he should have gone to live in such a dangerous country. (模考 91 年,

聯考 47, 63, 65, 66, 67, 86 年,學測 99 年,指考 92 年)

in	+	cred	+ ible
|		|	|
not	+	*believe*	+ 可以

indebted 〔 ɪn'dɛtɪd 〕 *adj.* 感激的

Thank you very much. I am *indebted* to you. (聯考 54, 69 年)

indifferent 〔 ɪn'dɪfərənt 〕 *adj.* 漠不關心的

We should not be *indifferent* to the suffering of our fellow countrymen. (模考 82 年，聯考 57, 60, 67, 69, 75, 85, 86 年，學測 94 年，指考 95, 96, 99, 100, 102 年)

indispensable 〔 ˌɪndɪ'spɛnsəbḷ 〕 *adj.* 不可或缺的

In my job, a computer is *indispensable*. Without it, I can't do anything in my office.

(聯考 72, 78 年)

individual 〔 ˌɪndə'vɪdʒʊəl 〕 *adj.* 單獨的

Each *individual* leaf on the tree is different.

(聯考 46, 66, 67, 68, 80, 83 年，學測 83, 84, 85, 87, 88, 91 ①, 98, 100, 101 年，指考 93 ①②, 94, 97, 100, 102 年)

industrial〔ɪnˋdʌstrɪəl〕adj. 工業的

Japan is an *industrial* country. (聯考 56, 61, 63, 64, 77, 83, 87 年，學測 86, 88, 91 ①, 96, 98, 101 年，指考 91, 93 ①②, 95, 96, 98, 102 年)

industrious〔ɪnˋdʌstrɪəs〕adj. 勤勉的

Even the most *industrious* student sometimes gets tired of studying. (聯考 49, 53, 73 年)

inevitable〔ɪnˋɛvətəbl̩〕adj. 不可避免的

Death is *inevitable*; it comes to everyone.

(模考 91 年，聯考 53, 63, 67, 68, 89 年，學測 83 年，指考 93 ①, 94 年)

in	+	evit	+	able
not	+	*avoid*	+	可以

informative〔ɪnˋfɔrmətɪv〕adj. 知識性的

These days some programs on TV are not only *informative* but also very enjoyable.

(聯考 73 年，學測 99, 102 年)

initial 〔 ɪˈnɪʃəl 〕 *adj.* 最初的

My *initial* offer was rejected. But I tried again, and it was gladly accepted. (模考 91 年，

聯考 65, 73, 82, 89 年，學測 85, 99, 100, 101, 102 年，指考 91, 95 年)

innocent 〔ˈɪnəsn̩t 〕 *adj.* 無辜的

Is he guilty or *innocent* of the crime?

(聯考 48, 67, 68 年，學測 96 年，指考 91, 93 ①②年)

instant 〔ˈɪnstənt 〕 *adj.* 立即的

The medicine can give *instant* relief from pain. (學測 91 ②年，指考 95, 100 年)

intelligent 〔 ɪnˈtɛlədʒənt 〕 *adj.* 聰明的

A dolphin is an *intelligent* animal. (聯考 49, 52, 63,

65, 71, 73, 74, 81, 83 年，學測 87, 100, 102 年，指考 93 ①，94, 96 年)

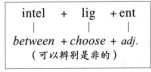

```
intel  +  lig  + ent
  |         |       |
between + choose + adj.
  （可以辨別是非的）
```

intelligible 〔 ɪnˈtɛlɪdʒəbḷ 〕 *adj.* 可理解的

Newspapers must be *intelligible* to all
levels of readers. (模考 91 年，學測 84 年)

intense 〔 ɪnˈtɛns 〕 *adj.* 強烈的

The *intense* heat in the desert is unbearable.

(學測 88, 90, 97, 99, 100 年，指考 93 ①, 94, 96, 97 年)

intensive 〔 ɪnˈtɛnsɪv 〕 *adj.* 密集的

She joined in an *intensive* course in English
writing. (模考 91 年，學測 91 ①, 92 ②, 100 年，指考 99 年)

intimate 〔ˈɪntəmɪt 〕 *adj.* 親密的

A few *intimate* friends are better than many
whose faces are all you know. (模考 83, 91 年，

聯考 68, 81, 83, 85 年，學測 85, 86, 87, 92 ①, 97 年，指考 96, 97 年)

invalid 〔 ɪnˈvælɪd 〕 *adj.* 無效的

Your driver's license expired last week and
is now *invalid*.

- [ ] initial _____
- [ ] intense _____
- [ ] impressive _____
- [ ] incredible _____
- [ ] impartial _____

- [ ] indifferent _____
- [ ] inevitable _____
- [ ] imaginative _____
- [ ] inadequate _____
- [ ] intelligible _____

- [ ] indispensable _____
- [ ] instant _____
- [ ] invalid _____
- [ ] industrious _____
- [ ] intimate _____

Check List

1. 單獨的   i   _individual_   l
2. 可理解的   i _____ e
3. 感激的   i _____ d
4. 不耐煩的   i _____ t
5. 不合的   i _____ e

6. 公平的   i _____ l
7. 工業的   i _____ l
8. 不足的   i _____ e
9. 勤勉的   i _____ s
10. 知識性的   i _____ e

11. 聰明的   i _____ t
12. 密集的   i _____ e
13. 無辜的   i _____ t
14. 無效的   i _____ d
15. 立即的   i _____ t

invisible ﹝ ɪnˈvɪzəbḷ ﹞ *adj.* 看不見的

Ultraviolet rays are *invisible* to the naked eye. (聯考 67, 77 年，學測 84, 92②年)

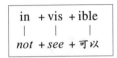

```
in  + vis  + ible
 |      |      |
not  + see  + 可以
```

irrelevant ﹝ ɪˈrɛləvənt ﹞ *adj.* 無關的

What the lawyer has said is *irrelevant* to this case. (聯考 66 年)

irritable ﹝ ˈɪrətəbḷ ﹞ *adj.* 易怒的

Peter has a quick temper. He is *irritable*.

(聯考 89 年，指考 92 年)

L l

lasting ﹝ ˈlæstɪŋ ﹞ *adj.* 持久的

My recent trip to Europe has left a *lasting* impression on me. (聯考 84 年，學測 86 年)

luxurious 〔 lʌg'ʒʊrɪəs 〕 *adj.* 豪華的

Nowadays many people drive *luxurious* cars to show off their wealth. (聯考 70 年，

學測 92 ②, 101 年)

M m

magnetic 〔 mæg'nɛtɪk 〕 *adj.* 有磁性的

Some animals are sensitive to the Earth's *magnetic* field. (聯考 48, 59 年，學測 98 年，指考 101 年)

magnificent 〔 mæg'nɪfəsṇt 〕 *adj.*
雄偉的

The castle on the hill looks *magnificent*.

(聯考 62, 64, 87 年，學測 96, 97 年)

magn	+	ific	+ ent
great	+	*make*	+ *adj.*

marvelous 〔'marvləs 〕 *adj.* 令人驚嘆的

This exhibition of Chinese paintings is *marvelous*. Indeed, it's the best in ten years.

(聯考 85 年，學測 94, 97 年)

mature 〔 mə'tjʊr 〕 *adj.* 成熟的

After three years' training, Mike has become a *mature* young man. (聯考 72 年，學測 100, 101 年，

指考 91, 96, 100 年)

medical 〔'mɛdɪkḷ 〕 *adj.* 醫學的

He has made up his mind to enter a *medical* school and become a doctor. (聯考 61, 76, 84, 88, 90 年，

學測 88, 92 ①②, 93, 97 年，指考 93 ①②, 94, 95, 98, 100, 102 年)

mental 〔'mɛntḷ 〕 *adj.* 心理的

Books and magazines are often referred to as *mental* food. (聯考 52, 53, 77, 81 年，學測 86, 102 年，

指考 99 年)

mere 〔 mɪr 〕 *adj.* 僅僅

What he described is a *mere* detail of the
plan. (聯考 47, 53, 54, 55, 63, 83, 87 年，學測 88, 96, 97, 102 年，指考 102 年)

mighty 〔'maɪtɪ 〕 *adj.* 強有力的

The pen is *mightier* than
the sword. (聯考 47, 75, 77, 90 年，
指考 101 年)

```
might + y
  |      |
力量  + adj.
```

militant 〔'mɪlətənt 〕 *adj.* 好戰的

Some *militant* members of the crowd started
throwing stones at the riot police.

military 〔'mɪlə,tɛrɪ 〕 *adj.* 軍事的

Every male in the R.O.C. has to perform
two years of *military* service. (聯考 67, 84, 88 年，
學測 88, 102 年，指考 96 年)

miserable (ˈmɪzərəbl̩) *adj.* 悲慘的

Many people in Africa live *miserable* lives.

(聯考 53, 69, 86 年，學測 102 年，指考 96 年)

moderate (ˈmɑdərɪt) *adj.* 適度的

What elderly people need is *moderate* exercise, not sports requiring great physical effort. (聯考 60, 73, 87, 90 年，學測 97, 99, 100 年)

moist (mɔɪst) *adj.* 潮濕的

The story was so sad that at the end my eyes were *moist* with tears. (聯考 61 年，學測 100 年)

monotonous (məˈnɑtn̩əs) *adj.* 單調的

He read the article in such a *monotonous* voice that we nearly fell asleep. (聯考 60 年，

指考 95 年)

mono	+ ton	+ ous
one	+ tone	+ adj.

mutual 〔'mjutʃuəl〕 *adj.* 互相的

Bill disliked the man immediately, and the feeling was *mutual*. (聯考 51, 86, 87 年，學測 99, 101, 102 年，指考 91, 93②年)

N n

naked 〔'nekɪd〕 *adj.* 赤裸的

To the *naked* eye, the Milky Way appears as a thin white cloud. (指考 98 年)

negative 〔'nɛgətɪv〕 *adj.* 否定的

The chairman gave a *negative* answer to our proposal. (聯考 57 年，學測 86, 91①②, 96, 97 年，指考 94, 100, 101, 102 年)

```
nega + tive
  |       |
deny  +  adj.
```

normal 〔'nɔrml̩〕 *adj.* 正常的

My *normal* working hours are from 9 am to 5 pm. (聯考 49, 51, 60, 66, 68, 72, 81, 84, 87, 89 年，學測 83, 86, 90, 91②, 92②, 96, 98, 99, 102 年，指考 93①, 100, 101 年)

自我測驗

- [ ] naked _____
- [ ] invisible _____
- [ ] irrelevant _____
- [ ] normal _____
- [ ] moist _____

- [ ] mighty _____
- [ ] mutual _____
- [ ] marvelous _____
- [ ] negative _____
- [ ] moderate _____

- [ ] magnetic _____
- [ ] medical _____
- [ ] military _____
- [ ] mental _____
- [ ] monotonous _____

Check List

1.	否定的	n _____*negative*_____ e
2.	持久的	l _____ g
3.	好戰的	m _____ t
4.	雄偉的	m _____ t
5.	豪華的	l _____ s
6.	易怒的	i _____ e
7.	有磁性的	m _____ c
8.	單調的	m _____ s
9.	成熟的	m _____ e
10.	僅　僅	m _____ e
11.	悲慘的	m _____ e
12.	心理的	m _____ l
13.	醫學的	m _____ l
14.	適度的	m _____ e
15.	無關的	i _____ t

noticeable〔ˈnotɪsəbḷ〕 *adj.* 明顯的

He was very shy, so his smile was barely *noticeable* when he met his teacher.

(聯考 48, 49, 50, 62, 75, 78, 79, 81, 82, 83, 84, 85, 86, 89, 90 年，學測 94, 97, 98, 100 年，指考 91, 94, 100, 102 年)

notorious 〔noˈtorɪəs〕 *adj.* 惡名昭彰的

The king was *notorious* for all his cruelties to the people. (模考 83, 91 年，聯考 63, 82 年，學測 89 年)

numerous 〔ˈnjumərəs〕 *adj.* 很多的

The stars in the clear sky are too *numerous* to count. (聯考 53, 58, 70, 79, 87 年，學測 85 年，指考 91, 94, 96, 100 年)

O o

official 〔əˈfɪʃəl〕 *adj.* 正式的

The president will pay an *official* visit to the U.S.A. (聯考 47, 48, 61, 76, 80, 82, 83, 84 年，學測 83, 91 ②, 94 年，指考 92, 93 ①, 98, 100, 101, 102 年)

original 〔 əˈrɪdʒən̩ 〕 *adj.* 最初的

The *original* locomotive was invented by Stephenson. (模考 83 年，聯考 53, 56, 72, 73, 82, 87, 88 年，學測 84, 85, 90, 91 ①②, 92 ②, 93, 94, 97, 98, 99, 101, 102 年，指考 94, 96, 99, 100, 101 年)

P p

passionate 〔ˈpæʃənɪt 〕 *adj.* 熱情的

We were all touched by his *passionate* speech. (學測 88 年)

passive 〔ˈpæsɪv 〕 *adj.* 被動的

The child was *passive*. He just sat there and waited for something to happen. (聯考 52 年，學測 86, 98 年，指考 95, 98, 102 年)

peculiar 〔 pɪˈkjuljə 〕 *adj.* 特有的

The koala is *peculiar* to Australia; you can't find it elsewhere. (聯考 68, 73 年，學測 83 年，指考 92 年)

permanent (ˈpɝmənənt) *adj.* 永遠的

The accident caused *permanent* damage to his brain. (聯考 45, 89 年，學測 86, 92 ①, 97 年，指考 93 ②, 95, 96, 97, 100, 102 年)

persuasive (pəˈswesɪv) *adj.* 有說服力的

Mr. Wang's arguments were very *persuasive*, and so his proposal was accepted. (聯考 55, 66, 79, 86, 87, 88 年，學測 86, 87, 92 ②, 94, 97, 101 年，指考 92, 93 ②, 95, 96, 101, 102 年)

pessimistic (ˌpɛsəˈmɪstɪk) *adj.* 悲觀的

No matter how difficult our national situation is, we have no reason to be *pessimistic*.

(聯考 68 年，指考 102 年)

poisonous (ˈpɔɪznəs) *adj.* 有毒的

After being bitten by a *poisonous* snake, he was rushed to hospital. (聯考 51, 70, 82 年，學測 92 ②, 102 年，指考 95 年)

populous 〔'pɑpjələs 〕 *adj.* 人口稠密的

India is one of the most *populous* places on earth. (聯考 85 年)

portable 〔'portəbl̩ 〕 *adj.* 手提的

We brought a *portable*
stereo with us when we
went picnicking.

(聯考 79, 84 年，學測 93, 98 年，指考 93 ②, 100 年)

practicable 〔'præktɪkəbl̩ 〕 *adj.* 可行的

I don't think your idea will work; it is not
practicable. (聯考 50, 67, 84, 90 年，學測 88, 101 年，指考 91, 94,
95, 102 年)

present 〔'prɛzn̩t 〕 *adj.* 出席的

At the meeting yesterday, some 300
members were *present.* (聯考 65, 66, 67, 68, 69, 70, 73, 76, 77, 78, 81,
84, 85, 86, 90 年，學測 84, 87, 88, 90, 92 ②, 100 年，指考 92, 93 ①, 95, 100, 102 年)

previous 〔'priviəs 〕 adj. 先前的

I'm sorry I can't go to your party. I have a *previous* appointment. (模考 83 年，聯考 62, 72, 84 年，學測 85, 86, 91 ①, 93, 96, 97 年，指考 96 年)

primary 〔'praɪˌmɛrɪ 〕 adj. 主要的

The *primary* purpose of this meeting is to reach an agreement between all of us. (聯考 51, 52, 75, 76, 88, 90 年，學測 83, 92 ①, 102 年，指考 92, 97, 99, 101, 102 年)

prim + ary
| |
first + *adj.*

primitive 〔'prɪmətɪv 〕 adj. 原始的

Primitive man made tools and weapons from sharp stones and animal bones. (模考 83 年，聯考 48, 54, 62, 68, 77 年，學測 93 年，指考 94 年)

proficient 〔 prə'fɪʃənt 〕 adj. 精通的

Prof. Black is *proficient* in English and French. (聯考 88 年)

profound ﹝ prəˋfaʊnd ﹞ *adj.* 深深的

I feel *profound* sympathy for your
bereavement. (聯考 87 年，學測 83, 85 年，指考 95 年)

prosperous ﹝ˋprɑspərəs ﹞ *adj.* 繁榮的

Have a Merry Chrismas and a *Prosperous*
New Year. (聯考 69 年，學測 90, 96, 99, 100 年，指考 99 年)

pro	+ sper	+ ous
forward	+ hope	+ adj.

punctual ﹝ˋpʌŋktʃʊəl ﹞ *adj.* 準時的

Mr. Nelson is very *punctual*; he is never
late. (聯考 47, 50 年，學測 98 年，指考 91 年)

R r

radiant ﹝ˋrediənt ﹞ *adj.* 容光煥發的

Alisa must be in love. She looks *radiant*.

(聯考 89 年，指考 102 年)

- ☐ radiant   _____
- ☐ present   _____
- ☐ passive   _____
- ☐ punctual   _____
- ☐ numerous   _____

- ☐ pessimistic   _____
- ☐ primitive   _____
- ☐ official   _____
- ☐ portable   _____
- ☐ peculiar   _____

- ☐ original   _____
- ☐ populous   _____
- ☐ proficient   _____
- ☐ notorious   _____
- ☐ persuasive   _____

1. 深深的   p _____profound_____ d

2. 很多的   n _____ s

3. 主要的   p _____ y

4. 被動的   p _____ e

5. 永遠的   p _____ t

6. 悲觀的   p _____ c

7. 可行的   p _____ e

8. 繁榮的   p _____ s

9. 明顯的   n _____ e

10. 特有的   p _____ r

11. 有毒的   p _____ s

12. 熱情的   p _____ e

13. 出席的   p _____ t

14. 手提的   p _____ e

15. 先前的   p _____ s

random (ˈrændəm) *adj.* 隨便的

When buying the lottery ticket, he chose his numbers at *random*. (模考 91 年，聯考 90 年，學測 101 年，指考 92, 98 年)

reasonable (ˈriznəbl̩) *adj.* 合理的

The price of the necklace is *reasonable*; it's neither too high nor too low.

(模考 83 年，聯考 56, 62, 63, 67, 70, 74, 75, 79, 87, 89, 90 年，學測 85, 86, 87, 88, 89, 91 ①②, 92 ②, 93, 94, 96, 97, 99, 101, 102 年，指考 91, 93 ②, 94, 95, 97, 98, 99, 100, 102 年)

reckless (ˈrɛklɪs) *adj.* 魯莽的

The report says that *reckless* driving has killed more than 20 persons since June.

(聯考 83, 84 年，學測 86 年，指考 98 年)

reck ＋ less
｜　　　｜
注意 ＋ 沒有

regular 〔ˈrɛgjələ〕 *adj.* 規律的

Regular exercise is essential to health.

(聯考 45, 76, 81, 85, 86, 90 年，學測 85, 86, 87, 88, 91 ②, 92 ①, 93, 94, 98, 101 年，

指考 91, 93 ①②, 94, 97, 99 年)

relevant 〔ˈrɛləvənt〕 *adj.* 有關的

Topics for conversation should be *relevant*
to the experiences and interests of the
students. (指考 94 年)

reliable 〔rɪˈlaɪəbl̩〕 *adj.* 可靠的

We got the news from a
reliable source.

(聯考 54, 65, 87 年，學測 96, 98, 101 年)

```
reli  + able
 |       |
rely  + 可以
```

reluctant 〔rɪˈlʌktənt〕 *adj.* 不願意的

Eva was *reluctant* to accept the challenging
project, but she was forced to.

(模考 91 年，聯考 52 年，學測 91 ②, 93, 96, 99, 102 年，指考 92, 93 ② 年)

remarkable 〔 rɪ'mɑrkəbḷ 〕 *adj.* 顯著的

She has made *remarkable* progress in her schoolwork. (模考 91 年，聯考 50, 57, 60, 71, 72, 90 年，

學測 88, 98 年，指考 94, 97 年)

respective 〔 rɪ'spɛktɪv 〕 *adj.* 各自的

The two brothers are studying in their *respective* rooms.

(聯考 53, 61, 83 年，指考 101 年)

respect + ive
|
方面 + *adj.*

ridiculous 〔 rɪ'dɪkjələs 〕 *adj.* 荒謬的

Don't you think it was *ridiculous* for these grownups to make such a fuss?

(模考 83 年，學測 91 ①, 101 年，指考 95 年)

rough 〔 rʌf 〕 *adj.* 粗魯的

Of all sports, American football is probably one of the *roughest*. (聯考 71, 72, 79, 87, 88 年，學測 85, 89,

96, 99, 102 年，指考 91, 93 ②, 96 年)

S s

sensible ﹝'sɛnsəbl﹞ *adj.* 明智的

He is too *sensible* to do anything foolish.

(學測 85, 98 年，指考 92, 93 ② 年)

sensitive ﹝'sɛnsətɪv﹞ *adj.* 敏感的

Alice is so *sensitive* that she is easily
moved to tears.   (聯考 85, 88 年，學測 85, 89, 93, 96, 97,

98, 100, 102 年，指考 100 年)

significant ﹝sɪg'nɪfəkənt﹞ *adj.* 重要的

The wedding anniversary of my parents
is a *significant* date in my family.   (模考 83 年，

聯考 66, 78, 87 年，學測 85, 94, 99, 101, 102 年，指考 96, 97, 98, 99 年)

slight ﹝slaɪt﹞ *adj.* 輕微的

I had a *slight* headache for lack of sleep.

(聯考 64, 66, 67, 68, 83 年，學測 94 年，指考 96, 100 年)

sober 〔'sobɚ 〕 *adj.* 清醒的

Make decisions only when you are *sober*.

solemn 〔'saləm 〕 *adj.* 嚴肅的

The teacher always puts on a *solemn* face;
however, he is kind at heart.

(聯考 68, 90 年，學測 89 年)

spare 〔 spεr 〕 *adj.* 空閒的

What do you usually do in your *spare*
time? (聯考 83 年，學測 91 ②, 99 年，指考 93 ② 年)

spectacular 〔 spεk'tækjəlɚ 〕 *adj.*
壯觀的

If you climb up to the peak of Mt. Jade,
you will find a *spectacular* view up there.

(模考 83 年，聯考 45, 90 年，指考 94, 96 年)

spontaneous 〔spɑn'tenɪəs〕 *adj.*
自發性的

After the disaster, many people offered *spontaneous* help to the victims. (聯考 88 年, 學測 83 年)

standard 〔'stændəd〕 *adj.* 標準的

The *standard* height requirement for candidates in the beauty contest is 160 cm.

(聯考 65, 71, 78, 88 年, 學測 86, 88, 92 ②, 94, 99, 102 年, 指考 91, 92, 94, 99 年)

steady 〔'stɛdɪ〕 *adj.* 穩定的

She was trembling with excitement but her voice was *steady*. (模考 83 年, 聯考 72, 76, 85 年, 學測 85, 91 ②, 98 年)

stubborn 〔'stʌbən〕 *adj.* 固執的

He is as *stubborn* as a mule. (聯考 49, 56, 69, 70 年)

自 我 測 驗

- [ ] rough   _____
- [ ] spare   _____
- [ ] sober   _____
- [ ] regular   _____
- [ ] random   _____

- [ ] stubborn   _____
- [ ] ridiculous   _____
- [ ] reliable   _____
- [ ] sensible   _____
- [ ] solemn   _____

- [ ] slight   _____
- [ ] reckless   _____
- [ ] respective   _____
- [ ] relevant   _____
- [ ] reluctant   _____

Check List

1. 標準的　　　s ___standard___ d
2. 壯觀的　　　s _____ r
3. 重要的　　　s _____ t
4. 不願意的　　r _____ t
5. 自發性的　　s _____ s

6. 顯著的　　　r _____ e
7. 穩定的　　　s _____ y
8. 合理的　　　r _____ e
9. 各自的　　　r _____ e
10. 嚴肅的　　　s _____ n

11. 荒謬的　　　r _____ s
12. 有關的　　　r _____ t
13. 固執的　　　s _____ n
14. 敏感的　　　s _____ e
15. 魯莽的　　　r _____ s

subjective〔səb'dʒɛktɪv〕*adj.* 主觀的

I don't quite agree with him. I think he is
too *subjective*. (聯考 50, 52, 54, 55, 65, 66, 74, 81 年，學測 83,

92 ①, 101, 102 年，指考 93 ①, 94, 95, 98 年)

sufficient〔sə'fɪʃənt〕*adj.* 足夠的

There is *sufficient* food for everyone. We
don't need to buy anything. (模考 83 年，聯考 88, 90 年，

學測 94 年，指考 91, 101, 102 年)

suf	+	fic	+	ient
over	+	make	+	adj.

suspicious〔sə'spɪʃəs〕*adj.* 可疑的

A man was hanging about the house in a
suspicious manner. (聯考 48, 72, 86, 89 年，學測 100 年，

指考 94, 102 年)

su	+	spic	+	ious
under	+	see	+	adj.

systematic 〔ˌsɪstə'mætɪk〕 *adj.* 有系統的

He worked out a *systematic* method of regulating clocks. (聯考 50 年,學測 100 年,指考 96 年)

T t

temporary 〔'tɛmpəˌrɛrɪ〕 *adj.* 暫時的

Temporary shelters must be built for these refugees. (模考 91 年,聯考 47, 50, 69, 73, 75, 83 年,學測 92 ①, 97, 99, 101 年,指考 91, 96, 97, 100 年)

thrilled 〔θrɪld〕 *adj.* 興奮的

We were really *thrilled* that our baseball team, Chinese Taipei, won the third place in the Baseball World Cup. (模考 91 年,聯考 81 年,學測 96 年)

timid 〔'tɪmɪd〕 *adj.* 膽小的

Johnny was too *timid* to jump over the gap.

(模考 91 年,聯考 61, 62 年)

tim	+	id
fear	+	adj.

tragic 〔ˈtrædʒɪk〕 *adj.* 悲慘的

The *tragic* sinking of this ship caused heavy loss of life. (聯考 80, 85, 88 年，學測 92 ①, 94, 96 年，指考 93 ②, 100, 101 年)

tremendous 〔 trɪˈmɛndəs 〕 *adj.* 巨大的

The typhoon caused *tremendous* damage to the crops. (聯考 46, 48, 71, 88 年，學測 91 ① 年，指考 93 ① 年)

tropical 〔ˈtrɑpɪkḷ 〕 *adj.* 熱帶的

Fruits like the mango, banana and guava only grow in *tropical* climate. (聯考 75 年，學測 88, 94, 98, 100 年，指考 96 年)

typical 〔ˈtɪpɪkḷ 〕 *adj.* 典型的

He is forgetful; it is *typical* of him to forget his umbrella. (聯考 51, 80, 90 年，學測 85, 92 ①, 93, 94, 97, 99, 100, 101 年，指考 92, 96, 97, 100, 101 年)

U u

unconscious 〔ʌnˈkɑnʃəs〕 *adj.* 無意識的

After he was hit by a car, he remained *unconscious* for half an hour before he came to.

universal 〔ˌjunəˈvɜsḷ〕 *adj.* 普遍的

The fear of growing old is *universal*.

(聯考 54, 67 年，學測 88, 90, 101 年，指考 94, 102 年)

uni	+ vers	+ al
one	+ turn	+ adj.

urgent 〔ˈɜdʒənt〕 *adj.* 緊急的

He was in *urgent* need of help. (聯考 48, 50, 65, 67, 85, 87, 88 年，學測 85, 86, 92 ①, 94, 101 年，指考 91, 95, 96, 98, 101 年)

V v

vacant〔ˈvekənt〕 *adj.* 空的

It is said that the house which has been *vacant* for several years is a haunted house.

(聯考 61, 79, 80, 82 年，學測 84, 89, 94, 99, 102 年，指考 97 年)

various〔ˈvɛrɪəs〕 *adj.* 各種的

There are *various* ways of cooking an egg. You can boil it, scramble it, or fry it.

(聯考 53, 54, 63, 77, 79, 82, 87, 90 年，學測 86, 89, 90, 91 ①②, 92 ①②, 93, 96, 99, 101, 102 年，指考 91, 92, 93 ①②, 94, 95, 97, 98, 99, 101 年)

vigorous〔ˈvɪgərəs〕 *adj.* 精力充沛的

Though over 70, my grandfather is still very *vigorous*. (聯考 60 年)

vital〔ˈvaɪt!〕 *adj.* 非常重要的

E-mail plays a *vital* role in modern communication. (聯考 64, 67, 78, 84, 87 年，學測 88, 90, 100 年，

指考 94, 98 年)

vulgar (ˈvʌlgə) *adj.* 粗俗的

Putting food into one's mouth with a knife is considered *vulgar* in England.

W w

weary (ˈwɪrɪ) *adj.* 疲倦的

The soldiers were extremely *weary* after 30 days of continuous fighting.

willing (ˈwɪlɪŋ) *adj.* 願意的

I am *willing* to lend you a hand. Call me when you need help. (模考 91 年，聯考 67, 73, 77 年，

學測 88, 91 ②, 101 年，指考 99, 100 年)

【劉毅老師的話】

Do you feel weary after memorizing so many words? Don't give up. Keep on trying. Be willing to sweat. I'm sure you'll achieve success in the long run.

自我測驗

- [ ] weary　　　_____
- [ ] typical　　_____
- [ ] vital　　　_____
- [ ] vacant　　_____
- [ ] temporary　_____

- [ ] timid　　　_____
- [ ] tragic　　_____
- [ ] vulgar　　_____
- [ ] willing　　_____
- [ ] tropical　_____

- [ ] vigorous　_____
- [ ] thrilled　_____
- [ ] systematic　_____
- [ ] various　　_____
- [ ] universal　_____

1. 緊急的　　u ___*urgent*___ t

2. 空　的　　v _____ t

3. 足夠的　　s _____ t

4. 可疑的　　s _____ s

5. 巨大的　　t _____ s

6. 無意識的　u _____ s

7. 疲倦的　　w _____ y

8. 暫時的　　t _____ y

9. 主觀的　　s _____ e

10. 有系統的　s _____ c

11. 悲慘的　　t _____ c

12. 各種的　　v _____ s

13. 粗俗的　　v _____ r

14. 願意的　　w _____ g

15. 膽小的　　t _____ d

★ 副 詞 ★

abruptly 〔 ə'brʌptlɪ 〕 *adv.* 突然地

The volcano erupted *abruptly*. (聯考 90 年)

absolutely 〔'æbsə‚lutlɪ 〕 *adv.* 絕對地

If you want to succeed in anything,
perseverance is *absolutely* necessary. (聯考 48,
58, 64 年，學測 91 ②, 94, 101 年，指考 93 ①, 95 年)

accidentally 〔‚æksə'dɛntl̩ɪ 〕 *adv.* 不小心地

The little girl dropped the glass *accidentally*.
She didn't mean it. (模考 91 年，聯考 50, 52, 65, 66, 67, 68, 71,
74, 80, 82, 85 年，學測 84, 85, 86, 87, 91 ①②, 92 ①, 93, 94, 99, 101 年，
指考 93 ①②, 94, 97, 98 年)

apparently 〔 ə'pærəntlɪ 〕 *adv.* 顯然

The four victims had *apparently* died of
carbon monoxide poisoning. (聯考 59, 67, 71, 84, 86 年，
學測 89, 97, 99, 102 年，指考 93 ②, 101 年)

approximately (ə'prɑksəmɪtlɪ) *adv.* 大約

The total sum of money we raised in the sale was *approximately* 500,000 dollars.

(模考 91 年，指考 91, 93 ①, 99 年)

```
ap + proxim + ate + ly
|      |         |      |
to  + near   + adj. + adv.
```

automatically (ˌɔtə'mætɪkəlɪ) *adv.*
自動地

When we approach the door, it opens *automatically*. (聯考 56, 63, 70, 87 年，學測 98 年，指考 95 年)

B b

barely ('bɛrlɪ) *adv.* 幾乎不

They kept silent, *barely* talking to each other. (聯考 54, 56, 59, 65, 67, 72, 77, 84, 89 年，學測 92 ②, 99 年，

指考 93 ② 年)

basically 〔'besɪk!ɪ〕 *adv.* 基本上

I *basically* accept your plan, but I think it should be somewhat reworded. (聯考 67, 85, 87, 90 年,

學測 85, 89, 90 年,指考 93 ①, 101 年)

bitterly 〔'bɪtəlɪ〕 *adv.* 激烈地

She complained *bitterly* when she heard that she had to work on Sunday. (聯考 52, 63, 66 年,

學測 94, 98 年,指考 95 年)

C c

casually 〔'kæʒʊəlɪ〕 *adv.* 輕便地

Mary is having a tough time deciding whether to dress *casually* or formally for the party tonight. (聯考 83 年,學測 84, 85, 87, 91 ①, 97 年)

closely 〔'kloslɪ〕 *adv.* 密切地

This problem is *closely* related to that one.

(聯考 68, 72, 74, 80, 87, 89 年,學測 84, 87, 89, 90, 92 ②, 93, 96, 97, 98, 100, 101 年,

指考 91, 93 ①②, 94, 97, 99, 100, 101 年)

consequently 〔ˈkɑnsəˌkwɛntlɪ〕*adv.*
因此

There was an oil spill off the coast; *consequently*, many marine species were seriously threatened. (模考 91 年，聯考 47, 53, 68, 78, 88 年，

學測 84, 88, 93, 94, 98, 102 年，指考 91, 92, 93 ①②, 95, 96, 98 年)

constantly 〔ˈkɑnstəntlɪ〕*adv.* 不斷地

Because Mr. Wang *constantly* changes his mind, it's very difficult to predict what he will do next. (聯考 48, 51, 54, 63, 67, 68, 79, 82, 89 年，學測 83, 88,

92 ①②, 98, 101, 102 年，指考 94, 96, 99, 102 年)

counterclockwise 〔ˌkaʊntɚˈklɑkˌwaɪz〕
adv. 反時針方向地

A tornado may whirl either clockwise or *counterclockwise*.

D d

definitely〔'dɛfənɪtlɪ〕*adv.* 確實地

This young artist's latest work was *definitely* better than any other work in the exhibition.

(聯考 55, 73, 83, 89, 90 年，學測 87, 90, 92 ① 年，指考 94, 98 年)

deliberately〔dɪ'lɪbərɪtlɪ〕*adv.* 故意地

I wonder why she *deliberately* turned up the radio when I was studying. (模考 91 年，聯考 67, 82, 83 年，學測 83, 89 年，指考 95 年)

desperately〔'dɛspərɪtlɪ〕*adv.* 拼命地

Mark has been looking *desperately* for the lost camera but he just can't find it.

(模考 91 年，聯考 61, 90 年，指考 93 ① 年)

directly〔də'rɛktlɪ〕*adv.* 直接地

She answered my question very *directly* and openly. (聯考 51, 66, 70, 83, 87, 90 年，學測 86, 88, 91 ②, 94, 96, 98, 99, 100, 101 年，指考 91, 92, 93 ②, 94, 97, 98, 99, 101, 102 年)

E e

efficiently 〔 ə'fɪʃəntlɪ 〕 *adv.* 有效率地

Working *efficiently* means doing your job well without wasting time or energy.

(聯考 48, 49, 60, 67, 69, 71, 78, 84, 86, 88, 89, 90 年，學測 85, 88, 91 ①, 94, 101 年，

指考 95, 97 年)

ef	+	fic	+ ient	+	ly
|		|			|
out	+	*make*	+ *adj.*	+	*adv.*

emotionally 〔 ɪ'moʃənlɪ 〕 *adv.* 感情地

Physically, Peter is well-built, yet *emotionally*, he is very weak and dependent. (聯考 79, 87, 88, 89 年，

學測 88, 91 ②, 96, 97, 100 年，指考 93 ①, 97, 98, 100, 102 年)

enormously 〔 ɪ'nɔrməslɪ 〕 *adv.* 大大地

With the investment in the stock market, his wealth increased *enormously*. (聯考 60, 65, 76,

82, 85 年，學測 84, 88, 91 ②, 96 年，指考 95 年)

自 我 測 驗

☐ accidentally _____

☐ bitterly _____

☐ directly _____

☐ abruptly _____

☐ barely _____

☐ efficiently _____

☐ desperately _____

☐ apparently _____

☐ definitely _____

☐ enormously _____

☐ deliberately _____

☐ casually _____

☐ closely _____

☐ emotionally _____

☐ constantly _____

Check List

1. 密切地　　c ____closely____ y
2. 絕對地　　a _____ y
3. 大　約　　a _____ y
4. 不小心地　a _____ y
5. 輕便地　　c _____ y

6. 故意地　　d _____ y
7. 不斷地　　c _____ y
8. 顯　然　　a _____ y
9. 自動地　　a _____ y
10. 拼命地　　d _____ y

11. 有效率地　e _____ y
12. 因　此　　c _____ y
13. 確實地　　d _____ y
14. 基本上　　b _____ y
15. 大大地　　e _____ y

entirely 〔 ɪnˈtaɪrlɪ 〕 *adv.* 完全地

In winter, the mountain is *entirely* covered with snow. (聯考 52, 59, 68, 70, 80, 84, 86, 87 年，學測 84, 92 ②, 97, 101, 102 年，指考 93 ②, 96, 98, 99 年)

eventually 〔 ɪˈvɛntʃʊəlɪ 〕 *adv.* 最後

With his patience and efforts, we are sure that *eventually* he will succeed. (聯考 51, 77, 84, 87, 88, 90 年，學測 85, 88, 90, 91 ① ②, 92 ①, 97, 101, 102 年，指考 95, 98, 100, 101, 102 年)

exactly 〔 ɪgˈzæktlɪ 〕 *adv.* 剛好

The doctor told him not to smoke, but he did *exactly* the opposite. (聯考 47, 49, 65, 66, 68, 74, 75, 76, 77, 83, 85, 89 年，學測 84, 90, 92 ②, 94, 96, 99 年，指考 91, 94, 96, 102 年)

extremely 〔 ɪkˈstrimlɪ 〕 *adv.* 極端地

Finishing the assignment in three days is an *extremely* difficult job. (聯考 52, 61, 63, 65, 66, 67, 72, 73, 77, 85, 86 年，學測 85, 87, 92 ② 年，指考 91, 92, 93 ① ②, 96, 97 年)

F f

firmly 〔'fɜmlɪ〕 *adv.* 堅定地

We *firmly* believe that with your intelligence and hard work, you will pass the exam without any difficulty. (聯考 64, 68 年，學測 87, 92 ①, 98, 100 年，指考 93 ①, 94, 100, 102 年)

forever 〔fə'ɛvɚ〕 *adv.* 永遠地

We are best friends, and I will cherish our friendship *forever*. (學測 89, 92 ②, 94 年，指考 98, 102 年)

fortunately 〔'fɔrtʃənɪtlɪ〕 *adv.* 幸運地

Fortunately, the drowning boy was saved by a soldier. (聯考 54, 69, 72, 86 年，學測 91 ①②年，指考 95, 96, 101 年)

frequently 〔'frikwəntlɪ〕 *adv.* 經常

Bob is *frequently* absent from work, which makes his boss angry. (聯考 81, 84, 85, 86, 87, 88, 89, 90 年，學測 85, 91 ②, 92 ①, 93, 94, 100, 102 年，指考 91, 92, 100, 101 年)

further 〔ˈfɝðɚ〕 *adv.* 更進一步地

I am exhausted; I can't walk any *further*.

(聯考 56, 62, 71 年,指考 93 ①②, 102 年)

G g

gradually 〔ˈgrædʒuəlɪ〕 *adv.* 逐漸地

The condition of the patient *gradually*
improved. (聯考 54, 57, 60, 62, 68, 70, 87 年,學測 86, 87, 90, 91 ①②,
98, 100, 101 年,指考 93 ①②年)

H h

hysterically 〔hɪsˈtɛrɪklɪ〕 *adv.* 歇斯底里地

As the singer appeared on the stage, her fans
screamed and shouted *hysterically*. (模考 91 年)

I i

immensely 〔ɪˈmɛnslɪ〕 *adv.* 非常地

At this historic site, you can see some
immensely magnificent palaces. (聯考 71, 87 年,

學測 83 年,指考 97 年)

impatiently 〔 ɪm'peʃəntlɪ 〕 *adv.* 不耐煩地

Several motorists were *impatiently* waiting for the light to change. (聯考 86, 89 年，學測 84 年，指考 93 ②, 95 年)

increasingly 〔 ɪn'krisɪŋlɪ 〕 *adv.* 逐漸地

It has become *increasingly* difficult to find suitable living environment. (模考 83 年，聯考 49, 59, 60, 61, 63, 67, 70, 72, 75, 76, 81, 83, 84, 85, 90 年，學測 84, 85, 87, 90, 91 ②, 93, 94, 96, 97, 98, 99, 101, 102 年，指考 91, 92, 93 ②, 94, 95, 96, 97, 98, 100, 102 年)

independently 〔 ͵ɪndɪ'pɛndəntlɪ 〕 *adv.* 獨立地

The main goal of education is to teach students how to think *independently*. (聯考 51, 53, 55, 65, 69, 72, 80, 86 年，指考 93 ①, 97, 101 年)

in	+ depend	+ ent	+ ly
not	+ *depend*	+ *adj.*	+ *adv.*

individually 〔 ˌɪndəˈvɪdʒʊəlɪ 〕 *adv.* 個別地

Group registrations are not allowed. Each member must register *individually*. (聯考 83 年，

學測 83, 84, 85, 87, 88, 91 ①, 98, 100, 101 年，指考 93 ①②, 94, 97, 100, 102 年)

inevitably 〔 ɪnˈɛvətəblɪ 〕 *adv.* 不可避免地

Technological changes will *inevitably* lead to a change in human relationships. (模考 91 年，

聯考 53, 63, 67, 68, 89 年，學測 83 年，指考 93 ①, 94 年)

intentionally 〔 ɪnˈtɛnʃənlɪ 〕 *adv.* 故意地

He broke the window *intentionally* to attract his parents' attention. (模考 91 年，聯考 46, 71, 86 年，

學測 86, 93, 98, 100 年，指考 91, 98, 101 年)

invariably 〔 ɪnˈvɛrɪəblɪ 〕 *adv.* 必定

Wherever he went, his funny action *invariably* attracted curious children.

(模考 83 年，學測 98 年)

in	+	vari	+	ably
|		|		|
not	+	*change*	+	*adv.*

M m

merely〔'mɪrlɪ〕 *adv.* 僅僅

He is *merely* a kid. Don't be too demanding.

(聯考 47, 53, 54, 55, 63, 83, 87 年，學測 88, 96, 97, 102 年，指考 102 年)

mutually〔'mjutʃʊəlɪ〕 *adv.* 互相地

Their opinions are *mutually* contradictory.

(聯考 51, 86, 87 年，學測 99, 101, 102 年，指考 91, 93②年)

N n

necessarily〔ˌnɛsə'sɛrəlɪ〕 *adv.* 必然地

Beauty is not *necessarily* a sign of a good
personality. (模考 91 年，聯考 46, 49, 52, 53, 58, 72, 73, 78, 83, 88 年，

學測 85, 86, 91 ①②, 92 ①, 97, 98, 102 年，指考 91, 92, 93 ②, 98, 99, 100, 101, 102 年)

nevertheless〔ˌnɛvəðə'lɛs〕 *adv.* 然而

She was exhausted; *nevertheless*, she
continued her work. (模考 91 年，聯考 65, 66 年，學測 84,

88 年，指考 91, 94, 95 年)

- [ ] immensely _____
- [ ] forever _____
- [ ] inevitably _____
- [ ] merely _____
- [ ] invariably _____

- [ ] extremely _____
- [ ] gradually _____
- [ ] increasingly _____
- [ ] further _____
- [ ] firmly _____

- [ ] mutually _____
- [ ] eventually _____
- [ ] nevertheless _____
- [ ] impatiently _____
- [ ] frequently _____

Check List

1. 僅　僅　　　m _____ *merely* _____ y
2. 幸運地　　　f _____ y
3. 逐漸地　　　g _____ y
4. 獨立地　　　i _____ y
5. 互相地　　　m _____ y

6. 極端地　　　e _____ y
7. 最　後　　　e _____ y
8. 個別地　　　i _____ y
9. 非常地　　　i _____ y
10. 故意地　　　i _____ y

11. 必然地　　　n _____ y
12. 剛　好　　　e _____ y
13. 必　定　　　i _____ y
14. 永遠地　　　f _____ r
15. 完全地　　　e _____ y

O o

obviously 〔'ɑbvɪəslɪ〕 *adv.* 顯然

He swallowed the food without chewing;
obviously, he was hungry. (聯考 49, 64, 76, 82, 83, 89 年，

學測 85, 96, 97, 98, 100 年，指考 91, 92, 93 ①, 97 年)

occasionally 〔ə'keʒənḷɪ〕 *adv.* 偶爾

It has only rained *occasionally* this summer.
The water we've got is not enough for this
area. (聯考 89, 90 年，學測 85, 88, 91 ①, 99, 101 年，指考 95, 98, 100, 101 年)

originally 〔ə'rɪdʒənḷɪ〕 *adv.* 最初地

Some minerals, for example coal and oil,
were *originally* living substances. (聯考 46, 53, 56,

72, 73, 79, 82, 87, 88 年，學測 84, 85, 90, 91 ①, 92 ②), 93, 94, 97, 98, 99, 101, 102 年，

指考 94, 96, 99, 100, 101, 102 年)

origin	+	al	+	ly
起源	+	*adj.*	+	*adv.*

overwhelmingly 〔͵ovəˈhwɛlmɪŋlɪ〕 *adv.*
壓倒性地

Yellow Stone National Park is *overwhelmingly* beautiful; it attracts numerous visitors each year. (模考 91 年，聯考 47, 89 年，指考 91, 95, 96, 102 年)

P p

partially 〔ˈpɑrʃəlɪ〕 *adv.* 部分地

What he said is *partially* true. (聯考 62, 87, 90 年，學測 92 ②, 97, 98, 101 年，指考 93 ①, 97, 101, 102 年)

precisely 〔prɪˈsaɪslɪ〕 *adv.* 精確地

The functions of this machine are described *precisely* in the handbook. (聯考 69, 71, 82, 84, 85 年，學測 90, 96, 99, 101 年，指考 91, 92, 93 ② 年)

previously 〔ˈprivɪəslɪ〕 *adv.* 之前

Peter couldn't attend the party because he was *previously* engaged. (聯考 62, 72, 84 年，學測 85, 86, 91 ①, 93, 97 年，指考 96 年)

primarily〔'praɪ,mɛrəlɪ〕 *adv.* 主要地

Today, we shall focus *primarily* on the
profits our company has made this year.

(模考 83 年，聯考 48, 51, 52, 54, 62, 68, 75, 76, 77, 88, 90 年，學測 83, 92 ①,
93, 102 年，指考 92, 94, 97, 99, 101, 102 年)

properly〔'prɑpəlɪ〕 *adv.* 適當地

Eat and exercise *properly*, and you will
stay healthy. (聯考 72, 74, 78, 87, 88 年，學測 86, 90, 91 ②, 92 ②,
93, 94, 99, 100, 101, 102 年，指考 91, 92, 93 ②, 99, 100 年)

punctually〔'pʌŋktʃuəlɪ〕 *adv.* 準時地

The students arrived *punctually* at 9 o'clock
for their English test. (聯考 50 年，學測 98 年，指考 91 年)

R r

recently〔'risn̩tlɪ〕 *adv.* 最近

The issue of environmental protection had
not received much attention until very
recently. (聯考 71, 77, 79, 80, 84, 85, 87, 90 年，學測 84, 85, 87, 90, 91 ①②,
92 ①②, 93, 96, 97, 98, 99, 101, 102 年，指考 92, 93 ②, 94, 95, 97, 99, 100, 101, 102 年)

regularly 〔ˈrɛgjələ‧lɪ〕 *adv.* 定期地

People over 40 should have a medical checkup *regularly*. (聯考 45, 50, 76, 81, 85, 86, 90 年，學測 85, 86, 87, 88, 91 ②, 92 ①, 93, 94, 98, 101 年，指考 91, 93 ①②, 94, 95, 96, 97, 99 年)

relatively 〔ˈrɛlətɪvlɪ〕 *adv.* 相當地

These questions are *relatively* easy. I am sure you can answer them. (聯考 47, 71, 88 年，學測 83, 87, 93, 96, 97, 99, 102 年，指考 97 年)

respectively 〔rɪˈspɛktɪvlɪ〕 *adv.* 分別地

My two sons, Adam and Alexander, are five and nine *respectively*. (聯考 53, 61, 83 年，指考 101 年)

roughly 〔ˈrʌflɪ〕 *adv.* 大約

The total amount of the damage is *roughly* 100,000 dollars. (聯考 71, 72, 79, 87, 88 年，學測 85, 89, 96, 99, 102 年，指考 91, 93 ②, 96 年)

S s

scarcely 〔ˈskɛrslɪ〕 *adv.* 幾乎不

When she arrived in the States, she spoke
scarcely a word of English. (聯考 63, 64, 65, 79, 86, 88,

90 年，學測 89, 96, 99, 101 年，指考 91, 94, 95, 97, 99, 102 年)

separately 〔ˈsɛpərɪtlɪ〕 *adv.* 各自地

After dinner, Richard offered to pay the bill,
but May insisted that they do it *separately*.

(聯考 64, 71, 78, 88, 90 年，學測 83, 86, 87, 96 年，指考 93 ①, 95, 102 年)

sincerely 〔ˌsɪnˈsɪrlɪ〕 *adv.* 誠心地

I *sincerely* congratulate you on your
passing the test. (聯考 68, 75, 86, 89 年，學測 85, 96, 98, 101 年)

T t

thoroughly 〔ˈθɝolɪ〕 *adv.* 徹底地

She cleaned her room *thoroughly*.

(聯考 49, 63, 66, 83, 84, 86 年，學測 83, 84, 97 年，指考 99, 100 年)

U u

unanimously 〔 ju'nænəməslɪ 〕 *adv.*

全體一致地

The committee agreed *unanimously* to carry out that project. (聯考 68 年，學測 89 年)

```
un  + anim  + ous  + ly
 |      |       |      |
one  + mind  + adj. + adv.
```

V v

vividly 〔'vɪvɪdlɪ 〕 *adv.* 生動地

She described the scenery *vividly* in her book. (聯考 72, 73, 90 年，學測 90, 98 年，指考 93 ①, 100 年)

自我測驗

- [ ] regularly   _____
- [ ] punctually   _____
- [ ] scarcely   _____
- [ ] respectively   _____
- [ ] obviously   _____

- [ ] precisely   _____
- [ ] originally   _____
- [ ] sincerely   _____
- [ ] thoroughly   _____
- [ ] separately   _____

- [ ] vividly   _____
- [ ] partially   _____
- [ ] roughly   _____
- [ ] primarily   _____
- [ ] unanimously   _____

Check List

1. 相當地　　r _____relatively_____ y
2. 之　前　　p _____ y
3. 適當地　　p _____ y
4. 生動地　　v _____ y
5. 幾乎不　　s _____ y

6. 顯　然　　o _____ y
7. 部分地　　p _____ y
8. 大　約　　r _____ y
9. 誠心地　　s _____ y
10. 徹底地　　t _____ y

11. 各自地　　s _____ y
12. 偶　爾　　o _____ y
13. 主要地　　p _____ y
14. 最　近　　r _____ y
15. 精確地　　p _____ y

★ 單字索引 ★

全書 328 頁

升大學必考 1000 字
1000 Key Words

附錄音 QR 碼 售價：220 元

主　　編 /	劉　毅
發 行 所 /	學習出版有限公司
	TEL (02) 2704-5525
郵 撥 帳 號 /	05127272 學習出版社帳戶
登 記 證 /	局版台業 2179 號
印 刷 所 /	裕強彩色印刷有限公司
台 北 門 市 /	台北市許昌街 10 號 2F
	TEL (02) 2331-4060
台灣總經銷 /	紅螞蟻圖書有限公司
	TEL (02) 2795-3656
本公司網址 /	www.learnbook.com.tw
電 子 郵 件 /	learnbook@learnbook.com.tw

2019 年 8 月 1 日新修訂

4713269383291

高三同學要如何準備「升大學考試」

考前該如何準備「學測」呢？「劉毅英文」的同學很簡單，只要熟讀每次的模考試題就行了。每一份試題都在7000字範圍內，就不必再背7000字了，從後面往前複習，越後面越重要，一定要把最後10份試題唸得滾瓜爛熟。根據以往的經驗，詞彙題絕對不會超出7000字範圍。每年題型變化不大，只要針對下面幾個大題準備即可。

準備「詞彙題」最佳資料：

背了再背，背到滾瓜爛熟，讓背單字變成樂趣。

考前不斷地做模擬試題就對了！你做的題目愈多，分數就愈高。不要忘記，每次參加模考前，都要背單字、背自己所喜歡的作文。考場不難過，勇往直前，必可得高分！

練習「模擬試題」，可參考「學習出版公司」最新出版的「7000字學測試題詳解」。我們試題的特色是：
①以「高中常用7000字」為範圍。②經過外籍專家多次校對，不會學錯。③每份試題都有詳細解答，對錯答案均有明確交待。

「克漏字」如何答題

第二大題綜合測驗（即「克漏字」），不是考句意，就是考簡單的文法。當四個選項都不相同時，就是考句意，就沒有文法的問題；當四個選項單字相同、字群排列不同時，就是考文法，此時就要注意到文法的分析，大多是考連接詞、分詞構句、時態等。「克漏字」是考生最弱的一環，你難，別人也難，只要考前利用這種答題技巧，勤加練習，就容易勝過別人。

準備「綜合測驗」（克漏字）可參考「學習出版公司」最新出版的「7000字克漏字詳解」。

本書特色：

1. 取材自大規模考試，英雄所見略同。
2. 不超出7000字範圍，不會做白工。
3. 每個句子都有文法分析。一目了然。
4. 對錯答案都有明確交待，列出生字，不用查字典。
5. 經過「劉毅英文」同學實際考過，效果極佳。

「文意選填」答題技巧

在做「文意選填」的時候，一定要冷靜。你要記住，一個空格一個答案，如果你不知道該選哪個才好，不妨先把詞性正確的選項挑出來，如介詞後面一定是名詞，選項裡面只有兩個名詞，再用刪去法，把不可能的選項刪掉。也要特別注意時間的掌控，已經用過的選項就劃掉，以免重複考慮，浪費時間。

準備「文意選填」，可參考「學習出版公司」最新出版的「7000字文意選填詳解」。

特色與「7000字克漏字詳解」相同，不超出7000字的範圍，有詳細解答。

「閱讀測驗」的答題祕訣

① 尋找關鍵字——整篇文章中，最重要就是第一句和最後一句，第一句稱為主題句，最後一句稱為結尾句。每段的第一句和最後一句，第二重要，是該段落的主題句和結尾句。從「主題句」和「結尾句」中，找出相同的關鍵字，就是文章的重點。因為美國人從小被訓練，寫作文要注重主題句，他們給學生一個題目後，要求主題句和結尾句都必須有關鍵字。

② 先看題目、劃線、找出答案、標題號——考試的時候，先把閱讀測驗題目瀏覽一遍，在文章中掃瞄和題幹中相同的關鍵字，把和題目相關的句子，用線畫起來，便可一目了然。通常一句話只會考一題，你畫了線以後，再標上題號，接下來，你找其他題目的答案，就會更快了。

③ 碰到難的單字不要害怕，往往在文章的其他地方，會出現同義字，因為寫文章的人不喜歡重覆，所以才會有難的單字。

④ 如果閱測內容已經知道，像時事等，你就可以直接做答了。

準備「閱讀測驗」，可參考「學習出版公司」最新出版的「7000字閱讀測驗詳解」，本書不超出7000字範圍，每個句子都有文法分析，對錯答案都有明確交待，單字註明級數，不需要再查字典。

「中翻英」如何準備

可參考劉毅老師的「英文翻譯句型講座實況DVD」，以及「文法句型180」和「翻譯句型800」。考前不停地練習中翻英，翻完之後，要給外籍老師改。翻譯題做得越多，越熟練。

「英文作文」怎樣寫才能得高分？

① 字體要寫整齊，最好是印刷體，工工整整，不要塗改。

② 文章不可離題，尤其是每段的第一句和最後一句，最好要有題目所說的關鍵字。

③ 不要全部用簡單句，句子最好要有各種變化，單句、複句、合句、形容詞片語、分詞構句等，混合使用。

④ 不要忘記多使用轉承語，像 *at present*（現在），*generally speaking*（一般說來），*in other words*（換句話說），*in particular*（特別地），*all in all*（總而言之）等。

⑤ 拿到考題，最好先寫作文，很多同學考試時，作文來不及寫，吃虧很大。但是，如果看到作文題目不會寫，就先寫測驗題，這個時候，可將題目中作文可使用的單字、成語圈起來，寫作文時就有東西可寫了。但千萬記住，絕對不可以抄考卷中的句子，一旦被發現，就會以零分計算。

⑥ 試卷有規定標題，就要寫標題。記住，每段一開始，要內縮5或7個字母。

⑦ 可多引用諺語或名言，並注意標點符號的使用。文章中有各種標點符號，會使文章變得更美。

⑧ 整體的美觀也很重要，段落的最後一行字數不能太少，也不能太多。段落的字數要平均分配，不能第一段只有一、兩句，第二段一大堆。第一段可以比第二段少一點。

準備「英文作文」，可參考「學習出版公司」出版的：